THE HAUNTING OF REDRISE HOUSE

GHOSTS AND HAUNTED HOUSES

CAROLINE CLARK

SPOOKY NIGHT BOOKS

Do not watch the petals fall from the rose with sadness, know that, like life, things sometimes must fade, before they can bloom again.

* * *

To receive a FREE short story The Black Eyed Children join my newsletter http://eepurl.com/cGdNvX

ctober 31st 1750

RedRise House

Yorkshire Moors

England.

10 pm

Alice knew it would be tonight. She was eight now. Sometimes it seemed that she had waited for this day for more years than she could count. Every year, on this night, they came for someone and tonight it would be her. She knew this wasn't logical. There were seven girls her age and it could be any one of them. Only, she knew it would be her. She felt it, and the fear was like a beast inside. Clawing to take control and to pull her down into its pit of dark despair. None of the other girls believed her tales. They said the missing ones had simply run away. Only there was no escape.

Alice knew, she had tried. She had been watching and one girl went missing this week every year. That had to be more than a coincidence. It had to be! Tonight, if she let them they would take her and she would never return.

The moon shone down through the thin curtains. Its silvery rays painted shadows across the walls. They were like monsters with long creepy fingers that pointed at her. Others were like the crone from the storybooks they were sometimes allowed to read. Bent and wizened and yet as powerful as the dark. She screwed her eyes tight to shut out the dancing figures created by the wind and the moon as it shone through the trees. Only, she dare not shut them for too long. If she fell asleep, she would lose and somehow she knew this was the battle she had to win.

Gradually the house grew silent. All the other children were asleep and she just had to wait for the hourly check and then she could make her move. In the darkness her heart beat in her throat and the blood rushed through her ears. How would she hear when they came if her head was filled with the sound of her own pulse?

The minutes passed so slowly and she started to get tired. Was Mary already asleep? Could she leave her? How could she have such a thought? Mary was just a year younger and if they could not take Alice then maybe they would take Mary.

Footsteps echoed down the corridor outside. They approached quickly and confidently. It would be the last check of the night. The one to make sure that they were all asleep. The lantern would shine over her and she must make sure that she did not blink, did not move and yet what if she had mistimed this? What if she had slept and the last check had already gone. What if this time the footsteps were the man in the hood? The one who would take her away.

The thought was so frightening that she felt sick and her eyes burst open. She had to close them, had to lay still and yet she did not think she could.

The door opened and the lamp light swung into the room. Footsteps approached the first bed. It was two away from her and she tried to close her eyes. They didn't want to shut but eventually she managed to force them closed. Only now she couldn't breathe. She had to breathe slowly and quietly and yet she was gasping for each breath. Almost hyperventilating in her panic. The lamp light flared which meant it was raised above the first bed. The footsteps had stopped as Matron looked down on Jennifer. She would be asleep, at only six she was always tired and often asleep just as her head hit the pillow.

The light was moving, coming closer and she held her breath for a few seconds. The light was over Mary's bed now and once more it was lifted. She crossed her fingers hoping that Mary would be asleep. That she wouldn't move and risk the belt. The lamp was raised and she screwed her own eyes down tight and took another breath. In the silence it sounded like a gulp and she knew she had to calm down. If they suspected then maybe they would take her now and then it would all be over. Who would save Mary if she were already gone?

The lamp lowered and the footsteps moved across the hard concrete floor. Each one was like a slap, slap, slap and Alice had to screw her eyes tight to not jump at every sound. Slowly she let out a breath and relaxed her eyes and face. This had to look natural. Matron was hard to fool and if she was found awake then the least of her problems would be the belt. It had happened only five times in her four years at the home. Each time had left deep welts on her buttocks and legs and as matron approached some of the scars began to itch. It was as if they could sense the belt, sense the punishment she deserved for defying her betters and staying awake.

Breathe, slowly, calmly. The footsteps stopped at the side of her bed. Through her eyelids, she could sense the light as it rose above her. How she wanted to gasp or breathe. To pull the thin and stiff blanket over her head and hide beneath its perceived safety but she must not. Stay calm, stay still as a dormouse.

In her mind she could see Matron. Her thin lips drawn tight over sharp pointy teeth. Her dark eyes sunken into her sallow skin. Her gray hair pulled back into a severe bun that stretched the skin across her bones making it look as if it would tear if she ever dared to smile. She didn't of course, she was always angry, always mean and yet after each disappearance she looked younger, more alive. Did she eat the girls?

Matron let out a breath and she almost jumped. The sound was coarse and phlegmy. Though she did not understand the consumption that was gradually killing the old woman, she sensed that her time was near. It made the old matron even more angry and prone to dish out punishment even when it wasn't warranted. Yet, Alice knew she deserved it tonight. She had defied them and forced herself to stay awake. What would be the punishment for that, if they knew?

Alice almost shuddered at the thought but she clenched her fists beneath the covers and kept still. Soon she would have to take a breath and then it would be over. How she wished that the matron would move away. Would go look at one of the other nine beds in this room or move on down the corridor to one of the other rooms.

The woman seemed to hesitate too long and Alice was sure

she had been caught. Any second now a hand would reach down and snatch her thin frame from the bed. Any second...

Matron coughed causing the lamp to shake in her hand and the light from it to bounce across her eyelids. Then she heard the slap, slap, slap as the footsteps moved away.

Slowly she let out a whistle of air and relaxed just a little. The footsteps were moving on, the lamp was fading.

Alice gripped tightly to her covers as Matron checked each bed and then she slap, slap, slapped back to the door and was gone. The footsteps faded down the corridor and went into another room. A yawn escaped Alice and she wondered how much longer she would be able to stay awake. They had worked extra hard these last two weeks. Scrubbing the massive house from top to bottom as well as working in the gardens and on the farm. There would be visitors tonight and so they had needed to prepare laundry and extra rooms. It was exhausting work and their rations had not been increased so they went to bed hungry each night and woke up weak for the following day's work.

Alice heard Matron approaching the door again. It did not bother her this time, as she would simply walk past and then go up the stairs to her own quarters. Once she heard her door close she would be sure that it was almost time. Maybe she would just give it a little longer. Enough time for Matron to get into bed and fall asleep. Did she sleep? Maybe she sat there waiting for one of the girls to move. Maybe she sat at the top of the stairs looking down and just waiting?

Alice pushed that thought away and concentrated on her plan. She intended to wake Mary and then go down the stairs into the basement. She knew where there was a lamp and a flint kept in the kitchen, she would grab it on her way out.

With that she would go to the basement where she had been told there was a tunnel that led out of the house and under the wall. If she could find it then they would escape and go somewhere nice. Maybe into the woods. They could live in a tree and hide from everyone who came near. It was a lovely dream and it filled her with hope. Just her and Mary safe and cocooned at the base of a tree. They would find mushrooms to eat and maybe catch rabbits and fish from the river. She had never caught a fish but how hard could it be?

Soon she would find out, for it was time.

* * *

"MARY, MARY WAKE UP PLEASE," Alice whispered into the little blonde girl's ear as she pulled back her lank and dirty curls.

Mary's eyes shot open, they were a pure blue and filled with fear. Alice placed a hand over her mouth before she could let out a squeal of terror.

"You are safe," she whispered. "It's just me, like I told you. We're leaving."

Mary rubbed her eyes and tried to keep them open. "I'm very tired and it will be time to get up soon."

"It's time now and then tomorrow you can sleep until dinner."

Mary's eyes opened even wider. The whites almost shone in the dark. "Really?"

"Yes, if... once we are out of here we can do what we want." Alice pulled back the covers and handed her a dress. "Only, hurry, we don't want to be caught. *Not tonight!*"

Soon they were sneaking from the room, their bare feet silent in the darkness. Alice knew her way to the kitchen. She had practiced counting out the steps for the last month. So she took Mary's hand and began to walk. The fingers clasped in hers were hesitant. They began to shake as the door closed behind them and the darkness settled over them like a shroud.

"It's ok," she whispered, "trust me."

Mary's arm shook as she nodded and Alice smiled into the darkness and began to count her steps. It was important that she kept her stride at the same length or she would miss the door. Twenty, then thirty just four more steps and she reached out for the door. Her hand banged into the wood and the slight sound seemed so loud in the darkness. Alice froze and listened.

There was nothing there and yet she thought she heard whispers from far away. Was someone else awake? Or were they already coming for her?

Quickly she searched for the handle and found it. Turning it in the darkness she slipped into the kitchen and reached behind the door. There on the side should be a lamp and flint. At first she could not find them and started to panic. She had never been in the basement. It was off limits. No doubt because of the escape route. Without the lantern she would never find her way and she would disappear tonight!

Then her fingers hit something hard and there was the sound of scraping. She had the lantern and then the flint. Almost letting out a yelp of joy she grabbed them and turned away from the door.

"Hold tight to my dress," she whispered to Mary. "I need my hands now. So hold tight and stay quiet."

"I'm frightened," Mary's voice was but a whisper.

Alice leaned in close to her and moved her hair so she could reply right into her ear. "Don't be, we will soon be free."

Then she turned and felt Mary's hand pulling on her dress. Together they snuck across the huge kitchen. The door to the basement was another twenty-two steps to their left. But she had to make sure she was central to the door before she started counting. Feeling the frame she got her position right and then with her eyes tightly closed she set off across the slate floor. At first she was rushing and knew the strides would be too long. Slow down, she told herself and adjusted her strides. She had counted this so many times she would not get it wrong.

Nineteen, twenty, twenty-one, they were so close she paused and listened. Her breath was coming fast and shallow and she was feeling a little dizzy. They were so close and soon they would be gone from here. Soon they would be safe. Twenty-two. She reached for the door. The unlit lantern in one hand the flint in the other. The flint scratched against the handle and she knew they were there. With the flint in her tiny hand she could not turn the handle and so she pushed it into the pocket of her dress and turned the handle. As she did she thought she heard whispers come from behind the door but they were gone so soon, she thought maybe it was just a gust of air.

Quickly, she pulled Mary through the door and onto the steps. They were stone and narrow and it was so dark but she knew she must shut the door before she lit the lantern. So she eased inside and felt Mary gasp as her foot missed a step. Using her body she stopped her falling and eased in a little further. It was so difficult in the dark. Before she had practiced, walking along the corridor with her eyes closed but here she was truly blind. Still it was not the time to turn back. She eased in a little more and felt Mary follow her. Reaching back she pulled the door closed and felt it click into place. They were safe. They had made it.

Feeling suddenly euphoric she pulled the flint from her pocket and struck it near to the lantern. It was something she had done a thousand times and light filled the stairwell.

She gave Mary a smile and was pleased to get one in return. Though the girl's face was pale and drawn she looked better than earlier.

"We just have to go down the stairs and to the left. There we will find a passage out of here."

Mary nodded and Alice led her down the stairs. They seemed to go on forever and she estimated that they were at least three levels below the house. Occasionally she thought she heard voices but decided it must just be the echoes from their footsteps. She tried to ignore the fact that they slap, slap, slapped on the steps as they climbed down and down. Matron was in bed, she had to be if they were to escape.

"How much further," Mary asked.

"Just a little."

Soon the sound of their feet was replaced by the rushing of running water. There must be a river beneath them and then they were at the bottom. There was a wide passageway and she could see water running through it directly across from them. She turned to her left and could have sworn she saw a flash of light. Maybe it was a reflection off the water. It didn't matter she was not turning back when they were so close.

Up ahead she saw a door and knew that must lead to the passage. Quickly she hurried towards it ignoring the cold and the ache in her legs. They passed an alcove filled with shelves lined with ancient books. With hardly a glance she rushed on, Mary still clinging to her dress. They both were afraid but it would all be worth it once they were free.

They reached the door and she turned around to smile at Mary. "We are nearly there. Soon you can sleep." As she said the words she knew she should have brought their blankets. Thin as they were, they were better than nothing. Why was she such a fool? Maybe she could get Mary to safety and come back.

Pushing the thought aside she reached out to grab the handle, before she could turn it she felt it move in her fingers and the door pulled away from her.

She stumbled into a large room. It was lit by flickering torches and rough hands pushed her into the center. Mary let go of her dress and she turned to search for her but fear dropped her to her knees.

They were surrounded by over a dozen men in long black cloaks and hoods. She had run straight into the very thing she was trying to avoid. As she turned to try and escape she noticed something behind the men. There were bones. Small bones about the size of her arm and legs and further around was something she couldn't believe. Was it real? Behind the men, in the darkest reaches of the room only just touched by the flickering light was a pile of skulls.

The men stepped back as if herding her towards that grisly pile.

Next to the skulls was a stone bench surrounding by flickering torches. *What was it for?*

Alice was grabbed from behind. One man clutching onto

each of her arms and hauling her from her feet.

"Run, Mary, run," she screamed as they carried her to the altar and lay her down on top of it. She tried to look for Mary as they held her down by her arms and legs, but it was not possible. No matter how she kicked and struggled she could not pull free. Their hands were so big around her skinny flesh.

Where was Mary, if at least she was safe then it didn't matter. As she tried to look for her friend, all she could see were two hooded creatures looking down on her. There was just a black emptiness inside the dark hoods.

For a moment she could not breathe and then they both raised their hands up to the hoods. The light flickered and all the lanterns seemed to dim at once. Alice knew that it was over for her and yet she was intrigued. She wanted... needed to see into their eyes to let them know that she was not afraid. That she had accepted this and that she would hate them for all eternity. As she had the thought she wondered where it came from. Was it even her own.

It didn't matter, slowly they pushed back the hoods.

Two pale faces were revealed. One a man of probably sixty the other was Matron. There was nothing remarkable about them until she looked up to their eyes... there was nothing there, just empty black hollows that seemed to suck her in and pull her down into a horror so great she heard herself wail.

In his left hand the man pulled a knife from beneath his cloak. It glinted in the darkness and suddenly she understood where all the girls had gone. They were here forever and soon she would join them. As the knife raised up above her she began to scream.

CHAPTER 1

*A*ugust 31st 2017

RedRise House

Yorkshire Moors

England.

10 O'clock

THE JOURNEY SEEMED to take forever and the longer the taxi drove down the winding lanes further and further away from reality, the worse Rosie felt. And yet in the same breath she also felt a great weight lifting from her shoulders. Why had she let Amy talk her into this?

"It's about another two miles," the cab driver called.

Rosie grunted non-committedly and kept looking out the window. It was beautiful countryside, rolling hills and gentle dales. They passed a dark green thicket of trees and a babbling brook ran alongside the road. The last house they had seen was over thirty minutes away but she had been told that the house she would be looking after was fully stocked and that she wouldn't need to go shopping.

It was a good job, she couldn't afford the taxi fare too often.

"You wouldn't catch me staying at that place," the cabby said.

Rosie half heard his words and assumed he meant because of the location. "I'm looking forward to some peace," she replied as a vision of anger and hatred filled her mind. It was followed by pain and her right hand reached up to the scar on her left cheek. For a moment she felt dizzy and a little sick. It was not just the ugly red blemish that just missed her left eye and traced down her cheek almost to her lip. That was bad enough but her right hand was puckered with burns. They no longer hurt so much that she wanted to scream but still they stung at times. She dropped her hand and pulled the fleece sleeves over it.

"Not sure you get it, did they tell you what happened there?"

Rosie hardly heard the words and she didn't want to talk. Nausea was overwhelming and the cab was hot and claustrophobic.

"I'm worried about leaving you," the cabby continued. "With what happened and all."

Rosie felt a jolt of anger. Yes she was a mess, scarred both physically and mentally but she could look after herself. This man had no right to judge her... how did he even know? Did he think she was having a breakdown? Or maybe that she was just too weak to cope. He had no right!

"I'll be fine," she managed through gritted teeth.

"You're not the first," he said as he pulled off the road and down a long driveway.

In the distance she could see the house. It was large and impressive if a little imposing. For a moment it reminded her of a stately home but as they pulled closer she realized it was smaller than that... though still very large. There were eight windows on each floor. Four either side of the door and the house stretched up three stories into the heavens.

The grounds were like a country park. All grass dotted with the occasional tree. There were copper beech, sycamore, a few massive and wizened old oaks and a few horse chestnuts. It really was beautiful. Then her eyes were drawn back to the house. The sun passed behind some clouds and for a moment it looked like a prison. Dark and foreboding. The windows were black and full of shadows and she felt a shiver go down her spine.

What was wrong with her? She was safe here. Clive would never find her. He would never even think to look.

"Like I said you're not the first. Maybe you should..."

"I don't need your interference," she snapped amazed at his audacity. She knew she was not the first woman to be attacked by their boyfriend. Not the first to be scarred but what right did he have to mention it.

"Lady, I just wanted to warn you."

Rosie felt her anger grow and as he stopped the car and looked back, the fire in her eyes stopped him in his tracks.

He nodded. "You have my number, call me if you need a ride. Don't worry what time of day or night it is I'll come for you."

Rosie didn't know what to think and she sat open mouthed

as he got out and unloaded her cases. Before he was done she stepped out onto the gravel drive and fumbled in her purse. Before she could find any money he shook his head and climbed back in the car.

"It's on the house, be safe and call me if you need me." With that he wound up the window and drove away. The wheels spinning in the gravel as he drove away a little too quickly.

For a moment all she could do was stand there and look down at the three suitcases and her laptop bag. This was now the sum total of her life and it felt a little pathetic. How had she let it come to this?

Then she was back in that night. It was almost exactly six months ago that her then boyfriend Clive Peters had forced his way into her flat. He had been getting more and more jealous over the preceding month and she had already decided that it was time to end it. That night, he turned up convinced that she was seeing someone else. Ranting as he pounded on the door. Her first instinct had been to not let him in. Only she was scared of complaints from the neighbors. Her rent review was coming up and the last thing she needed was to lose her home. So against her better judgment, she had let him in.

He was drunk. His dark good looks ruined by the angry red scowl that dominated his face.

"Where is he?" he yelled as he opened doors and ran through her place.

"Who?!" Was all she could manage.

The flat was not too big, just one bedroom, a kitchen come living area, and a bathroom and closet. Before long he had opened all the doors and checked every room. She was cooking up a pot of soup in the kitchen when he arrived. It simmered on the stove, just over boiling and the smell of chicken and stock seemed so at odds with such irate behavior.

"I know he's here," Clive ran into the kitchen once more.

"There's no one here." Rosie was unsure whether to be afraid or angry and was bouncing from one to the other.

"The man you're cooking for."

"Clive, that's just soup for the week. I cook up a big batch, and freeze some. You know this you've had it before." The anger was winning. She was tired and still had work to do. Placing a hand on his arm she started to guide him toward the door. "Why don't you go home now and we will talk about this tomorrow."

Before she even had time to think, he grabbed her hand off his arm and shoved it straight into the soup. The pain was white hot and seared into her very soul. In her mind, she was screaming as flesh melted down to nerves. Still, he held her hand in the pan forcing it down and down until it touched the bottom.

The world seemed to have narrowed down to just that arm. It filled her with an agony like none she had ever felt. For long seconds she was in a shocked and fugue state. Fighting against the hand that held her to no avail. Then she lashed out with her leg. It connected with his knee and he went down pulling her arm from the pan but also pulling the pan over and so it tipped down her chest and side, covering her in hot soup. In agony she fell to the floor kicking and punching out at the pain that controlled her.

Clive thought she was attacking him and reached for a knife. He slashed at her connecting with her cheek.

There was more pain but she also felt as if she was drifting. Sinking down and down into a nice and comfortable warmth that would soon cocoon her from the world. She closed her eyes and let go. There was one more pain, when he sunk the knife into her chest. Aiming for her heart the knife hit her sternum and bounced off, slicing down the side of a rib and into her lung. It collapsed the lung and she started to drown in her own blood.

As she gasped for breath, choking and coughing on her own blood, she saw him leave and closed her eyes. It was time to go, to leave the world.

Shaking her head she came back to the present and the reason she was here. Not two minutes after Clive had left, her best friend, Amy, came over and found her dying. She had saved her that night and now she had offered her a lifeline once more. Rosie had given up her flat. Clive had escaped custody and there was no way she was going back there. She couldn't stay with Amy, he knew where that was. So she had burned through her savings on hotels. Moving every few days since she had left the hospital.

Now her money was gone and she had nowhere to live. As an author, well she still didn't quite believe that, she could work from anywhere. Her first book had done ok and the deadline for the second was only two months away. Yet she could not write. Every time she heard a noise, a voice, footsteps, a car door, anything, she was a nervous wreck. That was why Amy had suggested this job. House sitting in a remote location meant that she shouldn't hear any of the sounds that normally turned her nerves to mush. At least that was what she hoped.

She closed her eyes and listened. The sun was shining and it felt warm on her face. There was the sound of a slight breeze and nothing else. Shouldn't there be birdsong? Maybe that was just in the books. Maybe the birds couldn't sing all the time. With that thought she picked up one of her cases and pulled the key from her pocket. It was time to see what her home for the next few months would be like.

Excitement coursed through her and it was the first time she had felt like that since the incident. Looking up, she nodded. The house had character. For a second she imagined a carriage and four horses drawing up outside. It would be black and beautiful with a crest on the door. The four matched gray horses pawed the ground impatiently but the driver handled them with ease and experience. A footman jumped down from the back and came around to open the door. In a beautiful yellow gown, a young woman was helped down and looked around. Her face lit up into a smile as she saw the house and the handsome gentleman waiting for her on the steps.

Yes, this house was going to be ideal. As a writer of historical romances, she knew it was perfect and would do wonders for her creativity.

Feeling better than she had in ages, she climbed the steps, unlocked the great oak door and stepped into a large and airy entrance hall. She wouldn't let the cab driver's words upset her. This was a new beginning and it was going to be great.

CHAPTER 2

*A*s she stepped through the door she let out a delighted gasp. The house was magnificent. A large entrance hall spread out before her. The floor was hardwood blocks polished to perfection with hardly a speck of dust in sight. How could she be so lucky?

The floor spread out before her leading up to a large central staircase. It was carpeted in rich deep burgundy. A three-foot spread of carpet was sentineled by two feet of dark wood, mahogany she thought. There was a thick crimson rope strung across the stairs as if to bar entry.

It made her chuckle for a moment but she passed over it and looked further around.

The walls were a rich cream and large portraits hung all around. There were several of a severe looking man and woman with lots and lots of children. *Must have been before television,* she thought with a chuckle.

Stepping a little further into the room, her footsteps echoed all around her and she did a little twirl, feeling rather ungainly with the suitcase. This place was just amazing. Perfect for her writing and so different to everything she was used to, it would surely ease her nerves.

Either side of her across the great expanse of the hallway was a door leading into a room and then in front of the stairs was a passageway, with the same wood block floor. She decided to explore those later, for now she turned to the door on her left. As she did, she noticed a small table to the left of the entrance. There was a large vase of flowers on it. *What a wonderful treat.* Quickly she walked across and admired the white lilies and pink and red roses that made such a beautiful display. Reaching out she took one of the blood-red roses in her hand. A sharp prick caused her to cry out before she could pull the rose to her nose. Ignoring the pain she breathed in deeply expecting the scent of a country garden. With a grimace she pulled the rose away. The scent was sickly, and reminded her of rotting flesh. Shaking her head she looked at her finger to see a drop of blood. The rose must still have its thorns. An old Chinese proverb came into her mind. "A thorn defends the rose, harming only those who would steal the blossom."

Maybe the house thought she was stealing from it... where had that thought come from?

The doctor had told her that the anxiety medication she was on could make her feel, one a little drunk, two confused, and three possibly suffer hallucinations. It had been a really reassuring conversation! Was this medication supposed to help or make things worse? Only, that was just her control issues talking. She hated to feel out of control and sometimes the tablets made her feel that way. Maybe she should ease up on them for a few days and see if the change of circumstances was enough to get her mojo back?

Still sucking the blood from her finger, she noticed an envelope in front of the flowers. It was cream, heavyweight paper with her name written in an extravagant script.

Miss Rosie Benson.

Picking it up, she turned the envelope over to see that it was sealed with a round red circle of wax with something stamped into it. Peering at the wax and feeling a little giddy at such a formal form of correspondence, she stared at the seal. That was what it was. One of those that used heated wax. Just like she wrote about in her own stories. Suddenly the idea came to her that she would have a romance through correspondence. Her hero and heroine would not know who they were conversing with until after they had fallen in love. It could be a historical version of *You've Got Mail*. She loved that film. Tom Hanks and Meg Ryan, there was just so much chemistry between them. Again she tried to discern the shape in the seal. It looked like a human skull but that couldn't be possible, could it? A shudder ran through her and her eyes would not leave the seal. What sort of people would have a skull as their seal?

Pushing the thought away, she slid her finger under the seal and broke the wax. Why did it look like blood? What was wrong with her? First she sees blood red roses, then she pricks her finger and now a blood red seal. It looks like she has become obsessed. Then she remembered back to the incident. There was plenty of blood and maybe it was understandable that she now saw it everywhere.

Deftly, she pulled the single sheet of paper out of the envelope. Once more it was written in an ornate script with a real fountain pen. Such lovely penmanship gave her an entirely new feeling. This one was of romance and old time courtesy. It took her back to an age where life was different, and in her mind, so much better. There were no cars polluting up the planet. No computers and phones constantly demanding your attention. It was a world where you could relax and be yourself. A world of charm and manners, of ball gowns and garden parties and suddenly she wanted to write again. Already this house had done her such wonders. Amy was right, this was the perfect place to finish her book and to escape the past.

The letter was still in her hand and as she looked down, blood from the rose prick had soaked into the beautiful paper. It looked like a crimson ink blot and filled her with despair. Such a beautiful letter and she had destroyed it. Was Clive right? Did she destroy everything she touched?

At the mere thought of him the scar on her cheek throbbed and the burns on her arm and chest flamed with heat. She had to stop this. It was simply the rantings of a bully and one who knew that she was about to let him go. It was just a way to hurt her and by allowing it to do so she gave him a power he didn't deserve.

Raising the letter she began to read.

Dear Miss Benson,

As you may well be aware, the house is owned by my wife and I, we are The Duncan's. We do not visit it regularly but Matron has been checking in on occasion. She is getting weaker now and needs to rejuvenate, hence your position here. Your job is to give the house a little life. To live here and ensure that its needs are met.

You have been carefully selected and we are sure that you will make the house happy. However, there are rules that we hope you will follow. As it is such a large house the upper floors are off limits as are the outbuildings. You are to live on the ground floor only and not to force any doors that appear locked. Matron has prepared a room for you to sleep in and one to write. They are opposite the library. The kitchen is stocked and will be kept filled with adequate supplies. Write anything you need on the list on the fridge door.

Matron looks after the place. She may pop in from time to time but it is unlikely that you will see her. If you do, please do exactly as she says.

Though I doubt we will meet on this side of the vale we hope you enjoy your stay and know that we will.

Yours sincerely,

Jeremiah Duncan

Rosie held the letter in her hand and almost let out a laugh. What a strange document. It was also a little creepy, but she had heard from Amy that this was not unusual. Amy spent her life house sitting for rich clients. She loved the job. Was always in a different location, always in a fantastic house and all her needs were paid for. Though she had mentioned that some of the clients could leave the strangest of requests. She had been asked to sing to the house plants. Only Gilbert and Sullivan songs. She had also been asked to put flowers on a pet's grave and read a chapter of a book a day to another grave, but at that job they never told her whose. It was creepy but she was paid well and the job was soon over.

Rosie turned the letter over in her hand. There was no mention of how long they wanted her here. She had been told it was an open assignment and that she would get more details as time went on. Well if Matron was ill then she guessed it would depend on when she was well enough to work again.

Folding the letter over and putting it back in the envelope

she left her case near the table and decided to fetch in the others before she explored.

Stepping outside the door she walked down to her cases. They were scattered around as if they had been kicked over by a petulant teenager. What had happened?

For a moment she just stared at the cases, her mouth open. Who could have done this? Then the old sickness was back in her stomach. *He had found her!* Looking around she searched for Clive. There was no cover close to the house. The trees were dotted about the grounds but there was nowhere for a car to be parked and it was too far from the road for him to have walked. Slowly she began to back towards the house. *What if he was inside?*

She whipped around, her heart pounding so hard that it tightened her chest and made it hard to breathe. Her hand went to the scar, her burnt hand and she was frozen on the spot. Then a breeze lifted her hair and she let out a laugh along with a great gust of tension. The wind had knocked over the cases.

Picking them up she went back inside and placed them on the beautiful floor. Then she shut the door. Taking one last look around at the grounds. They looked so peaceful, so beautiful and so well maintained. Matron must have had help. The house, what she had seen, was immaculate inside and so were the grounds. She hoped that it would not take her too long to keep it that way. Nothing must disturb her writing if she was to meet her deadline.

Closing the door, she locked it and placed the key on the table below the flowers. Now it was time to explore. Yet, her joy of the house was gone. Thinking of Clive had left her feeling sick and nervous. Would she ever escape his clutches?

CHAPTER 3

*R*osie spent the next forty minutes exploring her new home. The room to the left of the hallway was a library. It was wonderful, like something out of her novels. It was decorated in a mushroom color. The walls rich and the upholstery matching. The carpet was a similar color with veins of green running through it. There were several little sofas in a deep rich chestnut velvet spotted around the huge room, and against the sidewall, a huge fireplace surrounded by sofas, chairs, and a writing desk.

The room opposite was a large kitchen with an attached pantry. There were red slates on the floor. A huge range cooker and deep mahogany units. The sink was old fashioned and ceramic. The taps steel. When she turned them on the pipes rattled ominously for a few moments before spitting out some brown water. That was just what she needed!

Feeling a little despondent she held her hand on the tap as it vibrated from beneath the earth and then eventually the water ran clean. Maybe it was safe to drink? Maybe it had just been left for a while. She glanced around. The house was immaculate. There was not a speck of dust or a cobweb in sight. If Matron was ill she had done a very good job of keeping the place in order.

Turning she saw two doors. One was in the corner of the room and the other the middle of the same wall. She went to the left one first and found it was a pantry, fully stocked with jars, cans, and bags of everything from fish to flour. Much of it she would not know what to do with. In a panic she searched the kitchen. There was not a microwave in sight. More dread settled on her. It looked like she was going to have to cook. Then she spotted cans of beans, tuna, ham. Hopefully there would be bread, cheese, eggs, and bacon. She could manage omelets, sandwiches, and a good old breakfast. Looking out of the kitchen window, she noticed a small garden. There were lettuce and other salad vegetables growing. Behind the gardens were some old and dilapidated looking buildings. These must be the outbuildings mentioned in the letter. They were off bounds to her and she wondered if maybe it was because they looked a little unsafe. A few of the roof tiles looked loose and the roof itself dipped in the middle. Behind them was a woodland. The trees looked thick, dense and uninviting.

Then she turned to the door in the corner. There was a note on the door.

This room is out of bounds.
Do not enter.

How strange!

Rosie had always been one of those people who did not take well to authority. She had always been a rule breaker as a child, and seeing the sign made her hand reach down for the handle. It was old brass, darkened by many years and no doubt countless hands. As she touched it she felt a slight shock and pulled her hand back with a laugh. It had to be static... and yet the floor was slate. How would she build up any charge?

It didn't matter. She had the urge for a cup of tea and remembered seeing some bottled water in the pantry. It took her a while to work out how to light the range. She filled the heavy black kettle and placed it on the ring before finding the fridge. Pulling the door open she was assaulted with a smell of decay and stepped back. The door closed and the scent was gone. A groan escaped her. If all the food was rotten then how would she cope? Until she received her first pay check money was tight. With a feeling of despair she opened the fridge again. This time there was no smell and she looked in. It was stocked to the brim with everything she could need. There was meat, cheese, salad, vegetables, milk, and yogurts. The bottom half was a freezer and she looked in there to find lots more supplies.

The sound of the kettle boiling behind her made her jump and she let go of the door. With a laugh she turned away and made some tea. Strong and black just the way she liked it.

With the cup in her hand she explored the rest of the house. On one side of the stairs there was a large dining room, and a couple of box rooms. On the other she found her bedroom, a small bathroom, an office and a small sitting room. It was just perfect. So she set up her laptop in the office that adjoined onto her bedroom and opened up a document. For a moment, she looked around the large room. The office was painted in a deep russet. It should have appeared dark and depressing but instead it made the room look big and grand.

The drapes were an even stronger orange brown but deeply complemented the walls and there was a pale ochre rug on the polished wooden floor.

It was a sumptuous room with a large hardwood desk and an old-fashioned captain's chair. It was the sort of room she had sometimes dreamed of and here she was able to have it all to herself. Maybe it would help encourage her muse to put in an appearance. So she took a breath and looked down at the blank screen.

This was when she usually started to panic. To write she needed to be totally immersed in her story. There was no room for outside influence and thoughts but since the incident she could not let her mind go and truly relax. The slightest noise would force her back to the terrifying night. She would almost feel the force of the blows. Feel the skin melting as he shoved her hand into the boiling soup and then pulled the pan over onto her. Then her cheek would burn, a white hot pain just like the knife slicing through her tender flesh.

Shaking her head she pushed the thoughts away. She was torturing herself. Forcing the memories to come back when there had been no trigger. It was something her counselor had warned her against and she knew she had to stop it. So she took a deep breath. In and out, concentrate on nothing but her breathing and let her mind go blank. It took a while but before she knew it characters were popping into her mind and the plot of her book began to take shape.

Looking back at her laptop she began to type. Soon she had mapped out her main characters and set up the premise of a story. Of course her main characters hated each other in person but they were introduced in correspondence by a good friend. Her female character would be Henrietta Carter and her hero would be Miles Drake Browning. The minute she had given them names, they came to life in her mind and pulled her into the tale they wished to tell.

Henrietta was willful and disobedient but her family needed her to marry. Miles was jaded and bored with the same women who chased him for his wealth.

As the characters formed, her fingers flew across the keyboard. First she wrote out the character traits for all her key players. Giving each one a detailed life and characteristics. Then she wrote a plot. Over the next several hours she honed and built upon it until it filled her with excitement and joy. The happy ending was satisfying and yet not too predictable and she knew that she wanted to write this book.

As she saved the document it occurred to her that the room was dark. How long had she been writing? That very thought brought her out of her zone and she was instantly hungry. A quick look at her watch told her it was almost 9 pm and she hadn't eaten since breakfast. A laugh escaped her. She was back. This move had been the best thing she could have done.

Getting up from her desk, she pushed back the chair and realized just how dark the room was. Away from the laptop screen it seemed like a pit of gloom and for a moment she did not want to move out of the laptops comforting glow. A curl of fear appeared in her stomach and froze her to the spot. This was silly and she turned and headed for the door. That would be the logical place for the light switch. It seemed a long way and the further she got from the laptop the darker it seemed. It was almost too dark and she put her hands out in front of her. *What if something was there? What if someone was there?*

Ignoring her fear, she took another step and another. She had counted another six steps before her fingers found the wall. Then she started to search for a switch. The surface should have been smooth paint but it seemed to crumble under her fingers. The urge to pull her hand away was strong but she had to find the switch. Panic was waiting to consume her and if she did not bring light to the room soon she knew that it would win. Her breath was coming faster and faster. The laptop screen shone in the darkness but it was so far away. Had she really walked that far or was her vision starting to fade with panic?

Her hand scrabbled across the wall until it hit the doorframe. That had to be a good point of reference. She searched around the frame and her breath got faster, her chest tighter and her heart pounded so loud she could hear nothing else.

At last her fingers found the switch and she pushed it down. For a moment nothing happened and she heard a small cry escape her strangled throat.

What now?

Then glorious light flooded the room and all was back to normal. She had simply had a panic attack. A worthless one at that, for she could have pulled out her phone and put on the torch app at any time. That thought filled her with relief and a little guilt. How long had she been here and she hadn't even sent Amy a text to tell she had arrived safely. With the room flooded with light she went back to the table, saved her document and closed the laptop.

Leaving the room she found light switches as she went. They cast a yellow light duller but warmer than she was used to. It reminded her of years gone by before LEDs and the blue and harsh lights she had become used to. Once she arrived at the kitchen, she pulled out a pan and began to make an omelet. As it cooked she typed off a text to Amy.

'Sorry for not texting earlier. You were right this place is great. I will call you tomorrow but thanks and have a lovely night.

R xx'

The phone flashed back at her, no signal. Amy had warned her this could happen and yet knowing that she was so isolated hurt. What if something went wrong? Then she laughed. Wasn't that what she wanted all along? To get away from everyone. Dropping the phone back in her pocket she looked down at her meal. With the omelet, a salad as well as a glass of sparkling water all piled onto a tray she walked back to her writing room.

That thought excited her. For as long as she was here, she had a writing room and it felt good... amazing. Already she had been more creative than she had been in months. Maybe she could manage without the anxiety medication tonight? Maybe she should leave it a few days though? Amy was coming to visit for a few days at the end of the week and maybe that would be a good time to change her medication. Nodding her head in agreement she arrived back at the room and pushed open the door.

The light was off and the laptop screen lit up the room. A fission of fear stroked down her spine and her body went rigid. Stumbling to a halt she almost dropped the tray. As it slipped in her hands goosebumps rose on her skin and a stab of adrenaline jerked her arms righting the tray.

Slowly she reached out for the light and the room was flooded with brightness. *It chased away the shadows and all that could hide among them.* Where had that thought come from?

Slowly she approached the laptop. Surely she had closed it earlier and left the light on? When she had entered the room she had been positive but now, now she could not be sure. After all she was tired and on medication. Wasn't it entirely possible that she had forgotten to shut it down? Or that she had imagined doing so.

Sitting at the desk, she used the mouse, closed the document and powered the laptop off. This time she closed it and was sure she had done so. Next she put the tray on top of it and tried to tuck into the omelet, only her appetite seemed to have vanished.

CHAPTER 4

The sense of ease and comfort had left her. Rosie was back in her nightmare of fear and worry. Anxiety hung on her like a heavy cloak weighing down her shoulders and yet it offered no warmth; she shivered against the dread that seemed to lurk in the shadows. Though she knew this was stupid. It was just a mistake, she no longer wanted to be anywhere near that room. Closing the door to her *writing room*, she leaned a chair beneath the handle and shuddered. It was all in her mind. It had to be.

With a cup of honey-sweetened chamomile tea and a couple of ginger biscuits, she walked across the sumptuous rug towards her bed. The rug was soft beneath her feet and yet the blood red color and swirling pattern made her feel a little sick. She could not bear to look down at it. Shaking her head, she put the cup and saucer down on a bedside table that looked like it cost more than her book advance and climbed into the big four-poster bed. It was soft and comfortable, if a little cool. The crimson drapes were romantic and yet they felt like a trap. The comforter lay on her body, warm and yet oppressively heavy.

Stop it!

There was already a glass of water on the table next to her tablet box. Maybe she should take a sleeping tablet as well as her anxiety medication.

What could happen if I don't wake up?

Stop it!

Fighting against the gloom she took a sip of tea. It was hot and sweet, burning her mouth as it went down. Closing her eyes she decided to leave the lights on and get a good night's sleep. Everything would look different in the morning, in the light. So she opened the Kindle app on her phone and began to read.

Sipping tea, munching on biscuits, and reading a romance she couldn't imagine a better way to spend a night and yet her eyes constantly left the screen and searched the corners of the room. Her ears were poised for the slightest sound struggling to hear over the pounding of her heart.

Ignoring her paranoia, she read on.

The hero was a rogue and was currently mocking the heroine, yet the woman was clever and resourceful and turned his mocking right back on him. It was a lovely scene and she found herself chuckling. Beneath her voice there was the tinkle of piano keys. At first she didn't register what she had heard and kept reading. Then her mind thought it must be her imagination and a carry through from her reading. In the book, Charlotte the sister played the piano... only Charlotte wasn't in this scene. The sound came again, a discordant jumble of notes... not the masterful skill that Charlotte would use. Rosie jumped in the bed and dropped her Kindle.

What should I do?

There was nowhere to go. The text she had sent to Amy hadn't been sent. It was something she had been warned about, the house was remote and there was no signal.

If someone was here, what could I do?

As panic began to descend, she clutched onto the bed sheets. It was too far to walk anywhere. Should she hide or run? Maybe she should just stay still and hope that she was safe? Then she thought of the plucky heroine and felt a little foolish. Maybe it was the tablets messing with her mind... there was nothing to fear... surely. She had to let go of blaming every noise, every shadow on Clive. He wasn't here, couldn't be here. Maybe it was just the wind?

Convinced that the fear was all in her mind Rosie pulled on a robe and headed for the door. The feel of the rug beneath her feet was unpleasant. In her mind it was slimy and she lengthened her stride, feeling a great sense of relief as her feet touched the hardwood floor.

As she reached for the door handle, her breath was coming fast and hard. There had been no more noise. Or had there?

Would she hear it above her panting? With a hand poised above the age darkened brass she tried to slow her breathing. Taking a few deep breaths, she pulled herself back from the brink.

The past was gone. That was what her therapist had told her... Let the past go. Do not let it control your future.

There had to be an explanation for the piano. Maybe it was an auditory hallucination or maybe it was just the wind. Not really believing either of those options, she opened the door and listened.

Somehow, just moving had lessened her panic. The rushing of blood through her ears had slowed, her breathing was back under control. Earlier she had left the lights on low and she could see well enough. For some reason she didn't want to turn them up. It would give away that she was searching!

Moving silently down the long corridor she strained her ears. Turning her head left to right, holding her breath, she searched for any sound that she was not alone.

There was nothing. No wind, no creaking floorboards, no rustling of trees. The very silence was oppressive and seemed to weigh heavily on her shoulders. Though she wanted to turn and run back to the bed, she kept walking. Each step took her closer to the entrance hallway and the stairs. The more she thought about it, the more she knew that the noise had come from the second floor. The floor that was off-limits to her. Suddenly she wondered why. *Was something hidden up there? Was someone hiding up there?*

As that thought went through her mind, an image of Clive flashed across her vision. For a moment her legs weakened and she almost tumbled to the floor. Yet, the fear was soon replaced with anger. How long would she let him control her? How long would she live in fear? There had to be an explanation of what was happening and it could not be Clive. She had taken every precaution. There was no way he had found her, no way was he here.

Just one more step and she could see into the dimly lit

hallway. It was empty. The corners shrouded in shadows played to her imagination but she knew there was no one there. Somehow, she felt it.

To her left was the staircase. It was just out of her vision and she did not want to turn. Maybe if she didn't look then she would stay safe? And yet she knew she had to look. She had come this far, was looking for answers, how foolish would it be if she went back to her room without them? One thing was for sure, she wasn't sleeping until she knew what the noise was.

Slowly she turned towards the stairs. As she did a jumble of notes rang out almost simultaneously. There was nothing musical about them. In her mind she imagined someone angrily slamming their hands down on the keys.

With her heart in her throat she tried to swallow, tried to breathe and yet neither seemed possible. With knees too weak to run she wavered on the spot and waited. The silence filled the room and engulfed her. It seemed to wrap around her like a cold shroud and sucked the courage from her very bones. Yet, she could not do nothing! It was time to act or time to run. Swallowing once more she took control.

"Is anyone there?" she shouted at the stairwell.

The words echoed slightly, mocking her as they then disappeared into the dark emptiness.

The light from the hallway only lit up the first ten stairs. The rest were merely dark shapes and shadow. *What could be lurking amongst them? What would be hiding, waiting...?*

Slowly she approached the stairs. There was a crimson rope across them. It reminded her of the one they used at the theatre. The one to keep the crowds out. What did this one prevent from entering?

Shaking her head she took another step. Just past the rope on the wall was a light switch. If she got to that she could light up the stairwell. What would she do then? Just look... Would she have to break the rules and search upstairs? Surely that wouldn't matter. It was off-limits, surely they meant just to live, just to make things easier, unless of course there were secrets up there that they didn't want her to find!

Rosie knew she was letting her imagination run away with her and yet she could not seem to haul it back in. Images of beasts, ghouls, and monsters flashed across her mind and yet none of them were as scary as the one thing she was really frightened of... Clive.

The seconds were ticking by and there had been no more sound. Could it be something as simple as a draft?

"Is anybody there?" This time her voice was pleading and showed her fear.

As if in answer to her question a loud bang was followed by a discordant peal as if all of the piano's keys vibrated at once. The noises strummed across her chest bone and filled the house with cacophony before slowly fading away to nothing.

Rose's breath was held, her eyes wide, her mouth open, and her throat was suddenly bone dry. Every nerve in her body wanted to move, wanted to turn and run and yet, she did not know in which direction. Should she flee from the house and race back to the road? It had taken twenty minutes in a taxi from the nearest residents. How far could she walk, how far would she get if somebody wanted to catch her? The only other place was back to her room. She could wedge chairs beneath both doors and hide out until morning. That had to be her best option and yet still her legs would not move.

All she could do was stare at the darkness that hid the stairs. Then she saw something moving. Just a shadow, just a glimmer in the darkness and it was coming closer. Though still afraid she found herself walking forward. Before she knew it, she was standing at the bottom of the stairs and the darkness was getting closer. The hair rose on her arms and prickles ran down her back. Breath held, heart pounding, she waited.

Out of the darkness sauntered a sleek black cat and Rosie let out a laugh of pure relief.

How could she have been so stupid?

All this time she had tortured herself when there was a simple explanation. Though the Duncan's hadn't told her they had a cat. Maybe it slipped their mind. Maybe it was Matron's and she wasn't supposed to keep it. Or maybe it was just a visitor from time to time.

Orange eyes stared up at her and it let out a mournful meow.

Reaching down, she picked it up and hugged it close. It would be good to have some company.

"Okay Kittie, let's see if we can find you some food."

The warm body in her arms seemed to chase away the darkness. Carrying the cat, she walked back to the kitchen where she was sure she had seen some cans of tuna. It seemed strange that she suddenly craved the company of the beast when before all she wanted was solitude.

CHAPTER 5

The house felt peaceful and relaxing again. As she watched, the cat picked at the fish with such precision and dexterity. Making the simple canned meal look like a gourmet feast. Occasionally it would glance around at her. The orange eyes holding her in their gaze and she could not decide if there was gratitude or disdain reflected in them. Finishing the fish, the cat turned to a bowl of water she had placed next to it. It delicately lapped at the silvered liquid before sitting in front of the bowl. Then it began to clean its paws and whiskers.

As it worked, Rosie sipped at a glass of wine; she had found a bottle in the pantry. It was rich and fruity and a little stronger than she was used to. Already she was beginning to feel more relaxed, almost floaty, and she knew it was time to go back to bed.

"Well, Kitty, are you coming with me?"

The black cat stood at the sound of her voice and followed as she left the room. It made her feel good somehow. It was comforting in a way that she couldn't explain. Once they were back in the room, Rosie closed the door but did not put a chair beneath it as she had earlier. After all, the noise had just been the cat.

She settled down beneath the covers and was pleased when the animal jumped up beside her. It stepped across her and curled up in the crook of her knees. Through the covers, she could feel its small, warm body moving as it breathed.

The room was not completely dark. Despite finding the cause of the scare she did not feel comfortable without light and so she had left a small lamp on in the corner. It was comforting, a warm light unlike the modern spots that everyone seemed to favor. Maybe it was just because she enjoyed historical romance that this light seemed so much more real.

Snuggling beneath the covers, she began to think about her plot. It was a habit she had and could make it hard to sleep. Only tonight, her mind kept thinking about the house. There had to be so much history and she wanted to find out all about it. Maybe tomorrow she would have a look around. She could explore the grounds and who knows maybe she would even sneak upstairs and see what rooms were there. She could spend some time in the library. There had to be some documented history in the books held there.

Despite her excitement and intrigue about the property, she was starting to fall asleep. Though she fought against it, it was no use and soon she was drifting in that land just between sleep and wakefulness.

Voices intruded on her slumber. Somewhere close a man and woman whispered. This was not unusual for her. Sometimes as she fell asleep she would get into the minds of her characters. She would fall into a dream where she lived in their lives. If she was lucky, she would remember it in the morning and could use it in her work. However, most of the time it was just a fleeting memory when she woke.

The whispering was stronger now and closer and there was an urgency behind it that made her want to wake. Yet, sleep gripped her tightly, holding her down in its sweaty palms.

The whispers came closer and she could almost make out the individual words. It didn't sound like English but more like Latin and in the background she could hear someone chanting. Fighting against the lethargy of exhaustion she pried her eyelids open.

Standing before her was a man and woman. Perhaps her hero and heroine? They were wearing hooded cloaks. She imagined they had just arrived at the Manor House after a long carriage journey. The light was behind them and their faces were deep in the shadows.

This is a dream, she smiled... it has to be!

They do not return the smile. Instead they looked at each other and whispered once more. The words ran together and sent a chill down her spine.

"Invocatio veni nobis."

Though she knows this was a dream, must be a dream she could feel her fear building. A cold sweat broke out on her back. It was as if a force was holding her on the bed. Pushing her down and making it hard to breathe.

"Invocatio veni nobis," they said again and leaned closer toward her.

It was as if they were studying her, deciding if she was worthy.

Once more they looked at each other and this time they nodded.

Excitement and fear controlled her in equal measures. She knew she must move but she could not. She must see the dream through, it could be important.

They pushed back the hoods of their cloaks and she could see... black holes... there were black holes where there should be eyes.

A scream ripped her from sleep and she jerked in the bed kicking the cat across the covers.

Sitting up she clutched the comforter to her chest, breathing heavily and searching the room. It was empty, except for the cat who glared at her for disturbing his sleep.

Letting out a sigh, she realized that it was a dream after all. It felt so real, sweat was drying on her back and she was still shaking. As she looked around the room, a scent drifted across to her. One that curdled her stomach. It was Montblanc Legend... Clive's aftershave.

For a moment or two she let the tears come. Was this all just a symptom of her tortured psyche? Just a way for the stress to release? According to her therapist that was a good thing. Right then she wanted to ring the woman up and let her have a piece of her mind. If this was good then she would hate to see bad!

Instead, she lay back on the bed and tried to calm her breathing. It was time to relax. Reaching over she picked up her pill container and took out a sleeping tablet. It was late. Glancing at her watch she could see it was almost 2 in the morning. She was exhausted and yet too wired and afraid to sleep. Popping a pill, she swallowed it quickly, before she could change her mind.

Usually she didn't dream with the tablets. Maybe they would leave her a little tired and drugged in the morning... but that was better than another session with the creepy empty-eyed couple.

Lying back on the bed, she felt the cat jump up. This time it moved to the opposite side of the bed and circled a few times before lying down staring straight at her. Orange eyes accused her of treachery, and she almost laughed.

"Some friend you are," she managed and the cat closed its eyes and seemed to be instantly asleep.

If only!

Rosie lay there trying to think of her book and to get involved in the story. If she could do it, then her mind would relax and she would soon be tired. Yet, it was so hard. Everything had felt so real and yet it couldn't be. Gradually the minutes turned to hours as she tossed and turned on the bed. Each time she started to drift, she saw the couple before her in the most vivid detail and she jerked back awake.

At least it appeared that her imagination was working well. Fingers crossed, she should be able to get plenty of writing done tomorrow and yet she knew that was just a wish. Being this tired she would be lucky if she could string a sentence together.

Sighing, she rolled over once more. The cat raised its ears and stared at her dolefully.

"I know," she snapped and it simply closed its eyes and turned away from her.

Typical.

Closing her own eyes, she started to drift but then something yanked her back to the room and this time it was not the dream. There were no visions of people in hoods and no scent of aftershave. A noise had woken her and she strained her ears while holding her breath to try and make out exactly what it was.

Instantly awake her heart was pounding once more. Her pulse raced in her ears and the room seemed to buzz. It took but moments to realize that she was starting to hyperventilate and she slowed her breathing.

There it was again.

The sound of footsteps on the hard floor outside her room. No, not outside but further up the corridor. They were walking towards the kitchen.

Who was it?

Fear clawed at her throat and she started to choke. Then she realized that she had been holding her breath and she let out some air. The panic eased a little bit but still, she had to know who was in the house.

The sound of whispers could be heard all around her and coming from deep underground she could hear singing... no it was chanting... the sort you heard in horror films. It was the sound of devil worship.

For a moment she almost laughed. Her imagination must be running away with her. This had to be a dream. So she reached across and pinched her arm.

"Ouch!"

It left a red welt on the skin and looked real enough.

What should I do?

A child's scream pierced the night. Before she could even think she was up and running. Logical thought had left her, she could not leave a child in pain or distress. Maybe it was because the sound of a child crying had haunted her childhood. Many a night she lay awake listening to screams and cries through paper thin walls. Confused and scared, she would burrow under the blankets and cover her ears. She wanted to go get help, to tell someone but the shouting and screams frightened her so much that she could not even move.

Lying beneath the blankets she would stay as still as she could until the noise died down and she could breathe once more. By morning, she had convinced herself that it was just a nightmare and so she never mentioned it.

It was only after she grew up that she discovered the neighbor was hurting his little girl. Her parents had tried to help the little neighbor girl but no one believed them in time. Even now, some nights she lay awake wondering if she could have done more. If only she had gone to help. If only she had said something. Well this time she could. Maybe this time she could save a life.

Forgetting her own fear, she was at the door in just a few steps and out into the corridor without hesitation.

The scream still rang in the air and yet she knew it must have stopped. Quickly she ran along the corridor.

As she reached the hallway, she was grabbed from the side. Ice-cold fingers dug into her wrist and pulled her to a halt. Whipped around, she turned to face the same woman. The one with the dark cloak and the empty eyes. A gaunt face surrounded those eyes. It was pale and thin to the point of being almost skeletal. Though it was hard to tell her age, she had to be old and for a moment Rosie wanted to say, Matron!

The thought left her as the woman opened her mouth and began to scream a silent scream. A rush of foul air covered her and Rosie tried to pull back choking on the scent of decay. It was like rotten pond water, full of decomposed debris and accompanied by a festering stench.

The child's scream rang through the night once more. It was the sound of such fear and pain and she could not ignore it. Rosie fought to escape. She had to save this child. She had to, and she pulled with all her might.

The woman clung on to her wrist and Rosie felt a sharp pain. She stopped and looked down as she felt warm liquid wash over her hand.

Where the woman had hold of her was covered in red. Beneath the flood of blood she could see long black filthy claws of nails dug into her skin. They had sliced through her wrist and into her veins and her life's blood was draining away. It gushed from her wrists and poured onto the hardwood floor. It was too fast, too much.

Pulling with all her might, Rosie fought to escape. She couldn't remember why but she knew it was important. The nails loosened on her skin and she started to move. Elation filled her until her knees buckled. The sensation of floating was almost pleasant. A little like being drunk. Then she saw the floor coming up to meet her face.

For an instant she wondered if it would hurt. She never found out, for she was unconscious before she even hit the floor.

CHAPTER 6

*B*lood, pain, claw like fingernails, blackened and covered in blood. Her blood. Images flashed before her eyes and she was falling. Down, down, without the chance of stopping. Her heart had plunged before her and air rushed past.

"No!"

She woke with a start. Jerking up in the bed to see bright sunlight filtering through the thick drapes. The cat was curled up on the bed. It raised its sleek black head and stared at her with those amazing orange eyes.

Pulling her own eyes away, she stared down at her wrist. Expecting to see a gash there and the remnants of dried blood. There was nothing... nothing at all.

"What the..."

It must have been a dream. Just a dream. So much for not dreaming when she took a sleeping tablet. Slowly she got out of bed. Her pajamas were soaked in sweat. It looked like it had been quite a night. Quickly, she hit the shower. *Had there been a washing machine in the kitchen?* She couldn't remember but there must be, surely.

Soon she was dressed and she took her washing down to the kitchen followed by the cat. As the kettle boiled, she found the machine tucked away in the corner. It looked ancient but appeared to work.

The cat had finished his breakfast and was staring up at the door. Rosie opened it and looked out at the garden. It was lovely. Rows of salad and vegetables were surrounded by roses. Behind the garden were the outbuildings and to one side was a little table and chairs.

Making some tea and toast she stepped out into the garden. The cat was sunning himself near the table and she settled down to join him. It felt good to feel the sun on her face. This was what she needed. Once the toast was finished she leaned back in the chair and closed her eyes. The sun warmed her skin. It felt glorious. There was no noise, no banging doors, or squealing wheels. No angry piping or shouting of kids. It was peaceful, there was nothing to disturb her. Nothing! There was no birdsong, no breeze. It was almost as if she was in a vacuum. Then she imagined the woman from her dreams. The empty eyes and black maw of a mouth. The prominent cheek bones that seemed to push against paper thin skin.

A shadow crossed her face and she opened her eyes with a scream.

"I'm so sorry." Standing over her, silhouetted by the sun was a man.

Rosie pushed her chair back and almost toppled over as she scrambled to escape. Why was she seeing him?

A hand reached out for her and she stepped back to avoid contact.

"I'm so sorry if I scared you. Please be calm. My name is Nickolas, Nick Aubrey. I'm the local priest."

"Priest!" Rosie stopped backing up and looked at the man. As her eyes began to focus, she stepped to the side to see through the sunlight. The man before her was around thirty with short dark hair and a friendly, if a little-amused smile. He was wearing an old fashioned black suit with a dog collar. He was a priest. "I'm sorry," she said and walked back to the table. Her hand went to the scar on her face but she quickly pulled it away. "I must have been dreaming and I never expected anyone out here. It is so remote you see."

"I know," he said.

"Can I invite you in, offer you a tea? Or perhaps some cake?"

Nick looked up at the house and something crossed over his face. "Tea and cake would be lovely... but why don't we sit in the sunshine."

Rosie nodded. "Just give me a moment then," she said as she pointed to the seats.

Rosie almost ran back into the house. What was wrong with her, screaming because she had a visitor and all these nightmares? Maybe she had made the wrong decision. Maybe she should call Amy and leave? Yet it was only a few more days until her friend would come and see her. She could surely manage until then.

With the tea made and two slices of cake on plates, she took a breath and went back out to the garden.

"Here we go."

"Thank you," he said as he took the tray from her and placed it on the table. "How are you finding the place?"

"It's beautiful. I'm a writer of historical romance so a house like this is a dream for me." Though she said the words with confidence, she shuddered a little as she remembered just what those dreams were filled with.

"The taxi driver told me about you," Nick said. "I live not too far from here and so I just wanted to walk over and see how you were."

"That was very kind. I didn't know there were any properties nearby. It makes me feel a little better actually."

"Oh, has there been any trouble or anything strange happen?"

Rosie took a sip of tea and raised her eyebrows. *Did he know?* "No, nothing," she said and pushed the vision from her mind. "Please, eat your cake."

Nick picked up his cake and took a tiny bite.

Suddenly, Rosie was hungry. She guessed it must be stress or maybe the tablets she was taking. Though she had just had her toast, she took a bite of the cake. It was moist and delicious, but as she chewed, something wriggled in her mouth. Her throat tightened and the food lodged against her larynx. There she could feel something moving and she began to choke. The more she coughed the more her throat tightened and soon she was struggling to breathe. Tortured lungs screamed as tears came to her eyes. Though she tried to suck air nothing happened and her throat constricted even further.

Before she knew it Nick had put his arms around her and performed the Heimlich maneuver. As he squeezed, the cake was ejected from her throat and landed on the table. Crawling around inside of the gooey mess was a black maggot.

Rosie saw the insect and turned throwing up her toast and tea over the lettuce plants. Shakily she sank down into the chair. All she wanted to do was cry and yet, she would not break down in front of a stranger.

"Here."

She turned to see him handing her a crisp white handkerchief.

"Thank you... I ... I'm so sorry... what is that?" Clutching onto the handkerchief she wiped her mouth.

"Here, sip your tea. It will help."

He was kneeling at her side and holding the cup. Rosie took a sip but found it hard to swallow. *There was a maggot in the food!* She couldn't stay here, she wouldn't stay here... and yet she must. If she ran away again she got the feeling that she would be running for all her life. She had to make a stand. Maybe the food was just old.

"I know this was very traumatic," he said. "However, it is not as bad as you think. That was just a pantry moth larvae. They are harmless. All you need to do is throw away any food that is not sealed and wash the pantry with a mixture of water, vinegar, and peppermint oil. Then if you put bay leaves on the shelves it will help to deter the moths. Country living... I'm afraid it can be colorful."

"Bay leaves," was all she could manage as she thought about how her throat had closed up. How she had almost choked to death.

"Yes." He pointed across the garden at a green bush with rubbery looking leaves. "That is a bay, grab handfuls of the leaves and leave them around the pantry. You look quite pale, have you had any other strange experiences?"

Rosie wanted to tell him. To confess about the dreams and yet she didn't want to be judged. So far she had done nothing but scream in his presence and it mattered to her that he didn't think she was neurotic. "No, nearly choking to death on a pantry moth and being scared by a priest is enough for one day."

His laugh was a nice sound in the sunshine. "I imagine it is, but as I said, you are not the first and this is not an uncommon event in the country."

Rosie took another sip of tea and then topped up both of their cups. *How could he say that? How could such creatures be in the food in the 21st Century?* "Can you tell me a bit about the house?"

The smile slipped off his face and he returned to his seat. "What would you like to know?"

"As I said, I'm a writer and so any history could give me a flavor and an authenticity to add to my book."

"What did you say you wrote?"

"Historical romance."

"Well the house has a colorful history, but I'm not sure that it would suit your genre. You see it used to be a children's home, an orphanage I guess you would call it. Though from what I've heard a work house would be a better description. There are those who say that dark sacrifices were made in the basement. That it was a place used for devil worship."

"It has a basement?"

"Yes I believe so."

"Perhaps you can tell me more," she asked, for she felt that it was important. Maybe these dreams were her picking up on the energy of the house. Picking up on the residual pain that had been left there.

"I don't know a lot more to tell you, I'm afraid. I really just came here to make sure that you were all right. That nothing strange had happened. I was worried, you see."

"No, I'm fine," Rosie said and yet she was strangely disturbed by his manner. It was almost as if he wanted something strange to have happened.

"Then I should go and leave you in peace." He stood and looked a little ill at ease. "My home is less than a mile in that direction," he said pointing across the garden. "If you need anything, anytime day or night, come and see me."

"Of course, thank you and I'm sorry about the cake."

"Do not let it bother you. If I may, before I go, may I say a blessing?"

Rosie felt disturbed that he would ask and she did not know how to answer and so she simply nodded.

Nick turned and walked up to the house. As he stood before it, he made the sign of the cross and closed his eyes. "Bless this house, o Lord, we pray. Make it safe by night and day. Bless these walls so firm and stout, Keeping trouble and spirits out. Amen."

Rosie found the poetic rhythm of the blessing amusing. For a moment she had to suppress a giggle and yet as she watched him turn and walk away... the day felt just a little colder.

CHAPTER 7

The priest hadn't been gone for more than five minutes and yet Rosie could not face going back into the house. She had already thrown away the cake and the remains of the maggot ridden piece. It was not as easy to discard the taste... the feeling, and her stomach constantly gurgled at the very thought of it.

The priest's manner had upset her. He seemed obsessed with there being something wrong. If she let herself dwell on it, she would wonder if there really was something wrong with the house. Was there somebody here? Or was it something worse... was something wrong with the place... dare she think... was it haunted?

Shaking the thoughts aside she knew she had to do something. One problem with the creative mind was it liked to create. If she did not keep it busy her mind would find problems where there were none. She had been through so much. It was understandable that she was having nightmares. Maybe, it was even understandable that she was hearing and seeing things that simply were not there. Yet, as she sat here in this deadly quiet garden she could not shake the thought that she was being watched. Where were the birds? Why were they not singing?

Once more, she turned to look around. Trying to be as casual as she could and yet there was no one there. Why would there be?

Movement in one of the upper windows jerked her from her thoughts. She searched, where had it come from? It seemed to be the right corner of the house. Looking at it she felt uneasy. As if someone was looking back. As if they were hiding and yet it was impossible to see in. The light seemed to reflect off the window as if it meant to prevent her from discovering the secrets behind. Only this was just a foolish fantasy created by a tired mind. A mind that had been pushed to breaking point. Occasionally she saw shadows moving in the glass. The first time she had gasped and clutched onto her chest and yet soon, she discovered, it was just the clouds reflecting on the mirrored surface.

What was she to do? She sat there a few more moments and decided that there was at least one job that had to be done.

Getting up she walked across to what she hoped was the bay tree. It was shaped like a triangle. Neatly clipped and obviously looked after. The glossy leaves all perfectly cared for and it seemed a shame to pull them from such a beautiful plant. Then she thought about the maggot, the larva and how it wriggled against her tonsils. Reflexively, her body retched.

Ignoring the feeling she reached out for the bay leaves and pulled a few from the bush. The air was filled with the gentle fragrance of oregano or at least something a little similar. There was something about it that was clean and refreshing and she pulled off more and more leaves. Holding the bottom of her T-shirt, she filled it with leaves. The action of ripping them from the tree was cathartic and she started to feel better. Once she could hold no more, she set off back to the kitchen.

As she approached the door the inside of the house seemed dark and threatening and Rosie felt her feet start to drag. This was ridiculous! There was no choice, she had to go in there and clear out the mess. Of course she was dreading it, who wouldn't be?

Quickly she almost ran through the door. The house was cold but that was all she felt.

Dropping the bay leaves on the kitchen table, she then found some plastic bin bags and headed for the pantry. The house was quiet as if it was waiting and the air seemed charged with static.

Of course, it would just be her imagination. The thought of eating something that was alive... wriggling and squirming. Something that was dirty and rotten. Something that was more at home in decaying meat and food. It was going to take her a while to come to terms with that. An ache in her throat and a tightness in her chest brought it all back but she would not be controlled. She was stronger than this, she'd better get started on cleaning. Throwing out the food was the most productive thing she could do.

Once in the pantry, she tossed the coffee cake into a bag. Part of her wanted to open it up and see what was inside and yet if she did and it was riddled with maggots would she ever sleep again?

So she simply dumped it into the bag and then walked along the pantry throwing away anything that wasn't sealed in either tin or glass. There were flour and biscuits, currents and dried fruit, ham and some sausages, and a great big bunch of onions as well as many other items she did not even know what they were.

Once that was done she took the two full bags outside and dumped them in the rubbish bin. Now she could start cleaning.

With lots of soapy water she took everything off the shelves scrubbed everything down and then put it back. While she was working she felt better. As the time flew by all her problems were forgotten and just this simple movement seemed to ease all her troubles.

Occasionally, she thought she heard the piano. Only, when she stopped to listen it was gone. Once or twice she heard whispering and footsteps in the corridor. Again, when she stopped to listen there was nothing there. It had to all be in her head. Auditory hallucinations were all she could put it down to. After all, the medication she was on, along with the lack of sleep, was bound to mess with her head.

Once everything was cleaned, she filled a bowl with vinegar and peppermint oil, which she had found in a cupboard, and wiped everything down once more. The pantry smelled a strange mixture of the acidic vinegar all overlaid with what seemed like polo mints. It wasn't unpleasant.

Next, she spread the shelves and the floor with the bay leaves and then she put everything back.

It had taken several hours, her back was aching, her throat was parched and she was hungry but she could not face the thought of food. So she made herself another pot of tea and went back out to the garden.

The sun had risen past its apex and was sinking slowly down

the horizon. The day was still not cold and it was pleasant enough to sit outside. So she closed her eyes, sipped on the tea and tried to get back into her story. Soon, she would be writing again and once the story took over she could forget everything else.

It didn't take long for the characters to talk to her. Miles and Henrietta were corresponding by letter and each was describing the person they were expected to court.

Miles described her as an insipid and haughty creature who couldn't hold a conversation with a pack mule. The description delighted her and she could just see the handsome Duke penning the words in an elegant and yet, masculine script.

How could she have Henrietta describe him? Screwing her eyes tight she put herself inside the woman's head and transported herself back 200 years to Regency Britain.

In her mind, she was Henrietta who sat at a writing desk having just taken off her bonnet and gloves. She was breathless with excitement as she opened her correspondence and began to read. The letter delighted her and brought her out of her current gloom. Henrietta was chuckling aloud to herself at the thought of this poor insipid creature unable to keep up with the mule's conversation. She could almost see the mule raise its brown head. Big expressive eyes focused on the girl as it opened its lips in conversation.

The letter formed in her mind and she read it just as clearly as if it was handwritten in front of her. Then in her mind, she took a breath and pulled down an expensive piece of paper. Taking a bottle of ink and a quill, she began to write back. The first part of the letter was just Henrietta thanking him for his correspondence and telling him a little bit about her day. As the words formed, she couldn't resist describing the Duke that she was being forced to marry. The description flowed from her as if she was Henrietta and was in fact writing it at that very moment. *The Duke is pompous and conceited*, she wrote, and *more stubborn than any man I have ever known. He could possibly even be that Mule you write about.*

Rosie opened her eyes excited at the story. The words and images were flowing faster than she could remember and she knew it was time to start writing. Picking up her cup of tea, she rushed back to the house. This time there was no hesitation on entering. She was in full creative flow and it took over all of her thoughts. She almost ran to the writing room opened her laptop and navigated to the document. It was hard to keep everything straight in her head and her eyes were hardly on the screen until the document was open. Even then, she looked down at her notepad and began to scribble notes. Little bits about the conversation, bits about the dress and the house the atmosphere about how Henrietta was feeling. When she thought she had enough teasers to remember all she had imagined, she looked up at the laptop screen and almost fell off her chair.

Written across the page was just one word repeated over and over again and it chilled her blood to the bone. Die, Die, Die, Die, Die, Die, Die, Die, Die, Die, Die, Die, Die, Die, Die, Die, Die, Die, Die, Die, Die, Die, Die, Die, Die, Die, Die, Die, Die, Die, Die, Die, Die

There were pages and pages of it. Rosie felt a sharp pain in her chest and the hairs rose on her arms. She pushed her chair back wanting to get away from that awful sight.

What was happening? Who was doing this to her and why? Every instinct told her to run. To leave that place and run to the priest's house. Or to run back to the road and just get away from there. Almost in a daze, she began to stand but something stopped her. She had never run away from anything and she would not run now. There had to be a logical explanation for this. Maybe she typed one die and somehow the computer had just copied it. Maybe she was going mad or maybe somebody was messing with her. It didn't matter, she had run far enough, and it was time to make a stand.

Reaching out, she slammed the laptop closed intending to go do something else but what else was there to do? The house had no television. She had a phone with the Kindle app so she could read but she couldn't call anyone and right now she needed to talk to someone. The only people she could talk to were her characters so she had to face the story.

Her fingers were shaking as she reached out to lift the laptop up. The touch of the cold plastic sent a chill through her. Maybe she should go, maybe she was being foolish but she was stubborn and proud, and she would not give in. With a jerk, she opened the screen and stared defiantly at the page.

The words had gone. Staring back at her was a blank sheet with the simple words *Chapter 7* at the top. Panic reared up inside of her and her arms prickled as blood raced into them. Touching the mouse pad, she scrolled up and down. There was nothing but normal words and normal writing. All the way through the document she scrolled and then she checked her other documents but everything she opened was just as she had written it. Dropping her head into her hands, she sobbed. It was all in her mind. Nothing was wrong here except her.

It just had to be the medication. Only, if that was true how could she trust anything she did? Right then she wished more than anything that she could speak to Amy. Maybe she should walk across to the priest's house and ask if he could give her a lift to town. Yet, she felt so tired and decided all she could do was relax in the bath and get some sleep. Maybe tomorrow things would be better.

CHAPTER 8

*I*t was only three in the afternoon and yet, the thought of a bath drew her like a hungry dog to a bone. Maybe it would help her relax and she could get some sleep afterward. Maybe that was what she needed and all of this foolishness would drift away.

Hoping that she was right, she made her way back to the sumptuous bedroom and then into the bathroom. It was a small but lovely room. The walls were half paneled and painted in a battleship gray. A cast iron roll top bath stood on claw feet and dominated the room. The bottom was painted to match the walls, the floor covered in gray quarry tiles. It all gave the room a somber feel.

The sink and toilet looked old and antique and stood like soldiers supporting the bath. Next to them was a rack with towels, it all looked like a posh hotel room in some bygone age. Waiting for her, a lady, to enjoy the waters.

Quickly she turned on the taps and was pleased that the water ran clear. For one awful moment she imagined the black gunk that had come out of the kitchen taps the first time she used them. Luckily, that had gone.

As the water ran, she sat on the edge of the bath and poured in some bath salts. They turned the water almost blue, but again, it seemed to match the gray of the rest of the room. It amused her and yet also felt a little threatening.

What was wrong with her?

Even the color of the bath salts could make her ill at ease. Maybe she was having a breakdown? Maybe she should get help?

As the water ran, she pulled towels from the rack and put them to her nose. They smelt of mildew and rot and when she opened them up she could see where mold had grown in black dots across the cream thread. Dropping them to the floor she pulled back with disgust. *Could things get any worse?*

Tears formed in her eyes and she wanted to sink to the floor but she would not. She was stronger than this, so she went to the bedroom and pulled a towel out of her case. There was always a way around things and the easiest way here was to bleach the towels... or bin them.

That sounded like a good choice so she scooped them up and went to the back door. It was unlocked.

Had she left it so?

Unsure, she took the towels out and threw them on top of the rotten food. The bin was almost full and she had only been here such a short time.

For some reason that made her chuckle. What would her employers think? Here she was throwing away such a large amount of their stuff? There again, what should she think...

when everything in the house was rotten? It seemed sinister and yet maybe it was just that Matron had been ill for longer than they realized. She had simply let things get on top of her.

Locking the door, she went back to the bedroom and stripped off her clothes.

Stepping into the bath, she sank down into the luxurious heat of the water. It cradled her in soft warmth that lulled away the stresses of the day. Closing her eyes she slipped even lower and let her body almost float. The water caressed her shoulders and eased out the knots she hadn't even realized were there. Bit by bit, she began to relax and let go of all the things that had happened. It was foolish to dwell on them when they were probably all in her mind. It was time to recuperate and start again.

Before long, her mind wandered back to her book and the up-and-coming scene she was about to write.

Henrietta was preparing for a ball where she would have to dance with the mule of a Duke. Suddenly, she imagined the animal all dressed up for the ball. He would be wearing cream breaches with black boots and a crimson tailcoat. An extravagant cravat hung around the jackasses' neck and he batted his eyelids and twitched his big, brown and furry ears as Henrietta walked in.

She found herself laughing. It was good to escape into fiction and maybe she could use this scene to add a little humor to her book. Only it was time to get serious. The ball scene was one that needed careful thought and so she relaxed back and emptied her mind. Gradually, she worked her way into her character and became Henrietta. With her maid, she had chosen an empire gown in a royal blue with metallic trim.

With the extremely high waist and narrow shape it would suit her perfectly and would be matched with long white gloves that came past her elbows and a necklace of large stones that matched the color of the dress.

Rosie concentrated on creating a picture of the gown in her mind. Committing it to her memory so that when she returned to her writing desk she could describe it perfectly.

Henrietta was excited about the beautiful dress and going to the ball, but at the same time she wished she could share it with her secret pen pal. That, she would not have to spend time with the jackass.

Rosie laughed again and almost opened her eyes. The house was perfect for her writing and in between the patches of madness she was having so much fun. Maybe it was the atmosphere of the house. Or maybe she was just relaxing more but her mind seemed more creative and the words were flowing quicker than ever. If she could just keep control of her paranoia and these annoying hallucinations then she would soon finish this book.

It was only two more days until Amy arrived. Surely, she could hold it together until she did, then all of her problems would be solved. Amy had promised to stay for a few weeks. In that time, surely she could chase away these nightmares and return to some semblance of normality.

Dragging her mind back to the story, she began to plan the carriage ride to the ball.

She could almost hear the footsteps of the footman as she waited in the carriage full of excitement.

Something cold touched her head. At first she thought it was in her imagination but before she could react she was pushed beneath the warm water. Taken by surprise she opened her mouth to shout and hot water ran down her throat. Instantly, she was transported back to the present and a world of terror. Her lungs contracted and forced her to cough. At the same time she kicked against the bath trying to find something to push against. Her arms flailed against the side. Her legs against the base of the slippery tub as she tried to force herself upward and out of the water. It was all to no avail. Her lungs were bursting as she tried to keep her mouth closed all the time struggling against the force that kept her down.

The hand on her head was so cold. Ice traced down from that touch and threatened to send her into shock. Yet, she must not let it. Thrashing and kicking, punching and clawing she held her breath for her life and yet she knew at some point she would have to breathe in. When that happened her lungs would be flooded with warm scented water and she would drown.

At some point she opened her eyes and she could see dark figures above her. They surrounded the bath.

Kicking with all her might, she managed to raise her head above the water. At first she coughed and spat out a great stream of hot liquid. They were coming back at her and she knew she would be pushed beneath the surface so she drew in a long breath and held it.

Before she was pushed back under she could see they were wearing dark gray hooded cloaks and they were chanting. She could not understand what they said but she remembered it from her dream. She tried to see their faces but just before she was plunged back beneath the hot water she could see that there was just a dark hole beneath the cloaks. Fear squeezed her heart and filled her veins with ice just as she was forced back beneath the surface.

Once more, she was in a fight for her life. Thrashing from side to side kicking and clawing at the hand that held her. Nothing seemed to help, nothing seemed to work and the lights were growing dim. Her nails clawed at the heavy cloth but to no avail and despite her best efforts, she drew in a lungful of water. As it hit her lungs her body spasmed and tried to expel it. This was it! She was drowning. Her lungs screamed, her muscles ached and terror clenched tight on her heart.

Hot water filled her lungs and eased away her panic. Instead, she felt warm, as if she was floating. Was this it? Would she die here in this bathtub not knowing why? Not knowing if this was real or all in her mind?

The pressure was released and she floated back to the surface coughing and sputtering. The bathroom was empty. There was no one there.

Rosie sat up and leaned over the side. Retching so hard it felt like her lungs would come out with the water. All she had swallowed streamed out of her and onto the floor. Tears were running down her face as she coughed and spluttered and tried to draw in precious air. Gasping desperately, she leaned on the bath. Though she couldn't see. The room was black and filled with terrors. It took a moment or two before she could pull in enough air and the gasping slowed down. Gradually her vision returned and she searched the room.

It was empty, she was all alone.

Exhaustion took over. The adrenaline that had kept her alive was gone and she was beat.

Had she imagined this? There really was no one there.

As soon as she felt able to stand she climbed out of the tub and grabbed her towel. Stumbling, she ran to the bed and threw herself on it. Leaning back, she looked up at the ceiling. What was wrong with her? Had this happened? No, it couldn't have... there was no one here. Then something came to her mind. Was this a haunting? Was she just attacked by ghosts? For a moment she contemplated such a thing and then she began to laugh. It had to have been a hallucination. After all, it was still daylight. If these were really ghosts then surely they would wait until nightfall. Hot tears streamed down her face as she wondered if she really was going mad.

Part of her wanted to run from the house, to do anything to get out of there, yet she was so tired. Before she knew it, she had fallen asleep and for the first time in a while she did not dream. It was an exhausted, deep sleep and she woke a few hours later hungry and feeling refreshed.

At first she could not remember what happened, but it soon seeped back into her mind. As it did, she heard something above her. The sound of whispering, of soft footsteps. Was someone up there? Were they playing tricks? It seemed the obvious answer and she knew she had to find out. Part of her still wanted to run but she wouldn't. If someone was there then she would confront them and she would find out what was happening once and for all.

As she pulled on her clothes, her thoughts turned to Clive. Was it him? Had he found her somehow and was he trying to drive her mad? It was the sort of thing he would do and she knew that she should run. Only she had run enough. If this was Clive, then she would face him one last time, and God help her, she would win.

CHAPTER 9

*R*osie left the bedroom and the sound of whispering drew her towards the stairs. It was almost too quiet to hear and yet seemed to lead her on. Was she being sensible? She remembered the instructions from the Duncan's. That she should not go upstairs. Sensibly, she should not want to. If someone was up there, she should walk to the priest's house, Nicholas Aubrey, and get him to call the police and yet she felt compelled to go look.

Her shoes clicked as she walked down the hard wooden floor towards the entrance hall and the stairway. The noise made the house seems so empty, so hollow and her breath caught in her throat. What was she doing?

It didn't matter, still she was pulled towards the stairs and when she arrived at the hallway the black cat sat on the bottom step barring her way. Its orange eyes seemed to warn her away more than the crimson rope that was strung across the stairs. The eyes challenged her, warned her and yet she felt compelled to answer that challenge.

As she put her foot on the first step, the cat let out a mournful meow. Rosie stopped and thought she heard a whisper behind her. It was almost like the sound of a little girl, sneaking about in the dark. It chilled her blood and raised the hairs on her neck. She turned around but there was nothing there. The sun shone through the kitchen windows and the house seemed so normal, so beautiful and full of peace.

She should just go up and have a look. It was only normal, curiosity after all. Once more she put her foot on the step and the cat blocked her way. Maybe it just rushed towards her to rub against her legs. To demand attention and yet it felt very different. Pushing past it, she took another step but the creature leaped backward and struck out at her. Hissing, it swiped a claw at her leg. Sharp nails pulled at the heavy denim of her jeans and before she could react it clawed at her again. Rosie stepped back, a little perturbed. The cat seemed to relax and she reached down. Before it could claw at her hands she plucked it up and swept it into her arms.

"There, there," she murmured against its silky coat. "I'm not going to hurt you."

Gently she held it against her body and stepped over the crimson barrier rope.

The cat let out a mournful yowl and leaped from her arms. It landed deftly on the wood blocked floor and sprinted into the kitchen. Then it was gone and she felt all alone. It was as if the sun went down as the cat went out and the room felt a little colder.

Ignoring the cat, she began to climb the stairs. The deep crimson carpet was spongy beneath her feet. Obviously expensive and well cared for. The mahogany wood on each side was polished to perfection. There was not a speck of dust in sight. Yet the higher she climbed the thinner the carpet beneath her feet and the more run down the place began to feel. There was dust and cobwebs and in places the wood was scratched, the varnish peeling. Perhaps Matron couldn't climb the stairs; perhaps that was why it was so run down?

It was darker too.

As if the sun couldn't quite penetrate and chase away the gloom. Though she felt compelled to go forward, part of her wanted to turn and run. Yet she had to keep going, even though her footsteps had slowed and her heart beat against her chest like a warning. Little by little, she climbed until she made it to the top floor.

The corridor spread out both left and right. It was dark and gloomy. All the doors were closed and there were no lights. She looked around for a switch but couldn't find one. Maybe she should forget this? Yet something still pulled her onward. It was more than curiosity... was more like a compulsion. So she closed her eyes and took in a deep breath.

Which way should she go?

Left, she was pulled towards the left. Opening her eyes she stepped onto the landing and down the corridor. Cobwebs clawed at her face and she fought them away.

There were doors leading off each side. Coming to the first door on the left she tried the handle. It was loose and rattled in her hand. Yet it turned easily and she pushed the door open. It was lighter inside, yet still dim, as though the windows were dirty and could not quite let the sun shine through. The room looked like it had once been a bedroom. Pale faded peach paper peeled from the wall and hung down in tatters over a damp patch on the plaster. For a moment she thought it was skin hanging off the wall. Ignoring the hammering of her heart, she shuddered and shook the image away.

The floor was bare wood and covered in bits of old paper. There were six old metal-framed bunk beds. Three on either side of the room. Something about the room felt sad. It did not live up to her idea of the romantic mansion house that the lower floors gave her. No privileged lady would have lived in this room. Whoever had stayed here would be cramped and unhappy. She did not know why she felt that and yet she knew that if she closed her eyes she would see children. They would be hungry and cold and dressed in rags. Their large eyes pleading out of dirty faces beneath unkempt hair. At night they huddled together by the light of a single candle. They kept as quiet as they could and hoped that the door would not open.

She moved towards the window, her footsteps causing dust to rise and a cough escaped her. It echoed around the room in a most comical manner and her gloomy mood was broken.

Turning around on the spot, she sang the scale. Do, re, mi, fa, sol, la, ti. The notes echoed around the room and caught up with her own singing. She did it again, louder and with more gusto. It sounded like there were two of them and then three she carried on and soon she was laughing. After all it was just an empty house. A little run down, which made it a touch sad, but there was nothing more here.

The echoes had stopped and she was about to start singing again when she heard another voice. It was someone singing. A sweet voice that carried through the gloom. At first she was scared and yet it was just an old nursery rhyme. The sound must be traveling from outside. Perhaps someone was walking past.

She listened intently as the singing started again, louder now.

"Oranges and lemons say the bells of St. Clément's. You owe me five farthings say the bells of St. Martin's."

Rosie found herself smiling and imagined one of her characters paying for some oranges.

"When will you pay me? say the bells of Old Bailey. When I grow rich say the bells of Shoreditch, When will that be? say the bells of Stepney. I do not know say the great bells of Bow."

The room seemed to darken and she imagined a man in a prison cell. He was her and she was him, and dread hung on her shoulders like a wet blanket as she waited in the cold, dark cell for death to come. A sliver of light heralded company and grew as someone approached the door. It should have brought comfort and yet she felt her bowels clench as fear crushed her heart.

"Here comes a candle to light you to bed."

The candle stopped outside the door and she knew that it was there to tell her that tomorrow would be her last day; that it was over. Terror grew and her heart pounded like a steam engine. She wanted out of this.

The voice continued, haunting, and yet sweet, "Here comes a chopper to chop off your head, Chip chop chip chop—the last man's dead."

The words faded away and the singer was now humming the tune. Rosie shook herself. What was happening? Was this more from her tablets? Just a figment of her imagination?

After all that was a nursery rhyme of the time she wrote in. Perhaps she had researched it. Most nursery rhymes were based on terrible tales and her mind must be going back to her research.

Still, she heard the humming and was pulled towards the corridor and the source of the sound. Though her logical mind still believed it was someone walking past, she knew it was not. She knew that someone was in the house and yet she did not feel threatened. Disturbed and curious... but not threatened.

The humming continued and she was drawn like rats to the Pied Piper. The melodic and hypnotic melody pulled her forward.

The floorboards creaked as she crossed the hallway and turned towards the furthest room at the end of the corridor. It was the one where she had seen a shadow earlier. The one that gave her the feeling of someone watching her. As if with a mind of their own, her legs walked past room by room and on towards that dreaded door.

The closer she got the more she could discern the voice and she knew it was a young boy. It reminded her of choirs she listened to. Wide-eyed in awe at the perfection of the notes they sang and yet this simple nursery rhyme was filled with sadness. Tears were streaming down her eyes as she reached out to the door handle. Made of brass and tarnished with age. Cold to the touch she almost pulled her hand away, yet something forced her to turn it is as the humming continued.

She pushed the door open and could see a child. Just like she had imagined his hair was all a tangle. A dirty unkempt brown, it flopped across his forehead. Old-fashioned clothes were patched to the point of destruction. Though his chin was dropped almost to his chest, dark brown eyes pleaded with her and she could not hold their gaze. As she dropped her own, she noticed he reached out towards her with work worn hands that were covered in filth. Lowering her eyes in shame she noticed that his feet were bare and dirty and they did not touch the ground!

Rosie stepped back into the corridor, her heart hammered in her throat in time to the humming. The boy floated towards her, still humming.

Then he stopped, the noise faded and she looked up into those big brown eyes. They were filled with longing and hope and she wanted to run to him and pull him into her arms. Something awful had happened to this boy, she felt it.

Stepping forward he began to speak.

"Play with me?" he asked.

It was such a simple request and one she was happy to honor and she moved a step closer.

The child lifted his head, as she did hers; he spoke again.

"Play with me, please play with me. I'm so lonely. Why will no one play with me?"

Rosie could not see his lips moving. Where were the words coming from? As if in answer, he tilted his head back exposing his throat. A vicious slash mark cut across it and the words were coming from this ghastly opening.

Rosie turned to run. Behind her, blocking the doorway, were over a dozen children. All of them had terrible injuries to their throats. On some, blood ran down their necks and clothes. On others the wounds looked as if it they were old. Though the ragged edges were red, the wound no longer bled. The children were pale and drawn. Their eyes spoke of horrors she could only imagine.

Rosie gasped and tried to step back. There was nowhere to go. She was surrounded.

With blank faces and pitiful eyes the children reached out with grubby hands and surrounded her.

CHAPTER 10

ingers clasped onto her clothes. Tugged at her arm. Like digits of ice they chilled to the bone as the children herded her away from the door. Pitiful eyes pleaded for a moment and then they changed. Red appeared around the rims. The eyes turned white, opaque and sunk into tiny skulls. The children were animals. Coming for her with blood on their minds. Fingers ended in claw like nails. As dirty as if they had just torn their way out of the earth and were determined to drag her back with them.

Rosie turned in a circle. Panic flapped against her chest like a trapped bird as she searched for escape.

A noise started behind her. A shrill keening. She whipped around and she saw it was one of the children.

They were pushing her back. Towards the window. Their clasping hands, grabbing and poking, pushing and shoving. The sound rose until it hurt her ears and the panic fought inside of her. Like a beast trying to escape, it blocked her airways and squeezed her heart.

Louder, the sound grew. All the children wailed like a beaten dog and yet still they craved her blood.

Circling, herding, and pushing her backward.

Screaming.

Their mouths were all closed but the gash that was their throat opened obscenely. It vibrated along with the sound. That noise, that wail was of despair. It cut to her bone, sliced into her heart and made her feel all the sadness and torture they had suffered. Once they had hope. Not much. Just a little. Hope that life could be better. Only that hope had been snuffed out in a cold dark cellar that was damp and filled with water.

How did I know that?

It made no sense and yet she knew. She knew that they had died here, had been sacrificed and now they wanted her.

Why?

Still the noise rose higher and higher. She put her hands over her ears and pressed as hard as she could. The pain grew with the sound and she expected her eardrums to burst and blood to spurt out between her fingers.

"Stop it," she whispered but the torn and mutilated necks just flapped quicker, the noise rose higher.

Did they want her to save them? To put them to rest? Or did they want her to join them in their eternal hell? Backward and backward they pushed her. Forcing her toward the window and what—a fall to her death?

Rosie stopped as her legs hit the wood of the windowsill. Still they flocked toward her. Demanding that she give before them. The cold glass touched her back. She knew she had to fight, had to escape and yet how could she. There were so many of them. At least a dozen and they wanted her with them.

Why?

Grubby blank faces, opaque eyes and those hands kept grasping, kept pushing her back. Hands scraped across her clothes, nails cut into her skin and blood ran down her arms. All the time her heart raced so fast that she was sure it would burst.

"Keep Back," she called, but her voice was little more than a whisper.

The screaming stopped and first the boy, the one she had originally seen. The one with the brown hair that flopped across his forehead in a way that made her want to smile, started to hiss. It was a sound of disapproval and it set her nerves tingling.

"Hisssssssssssssss."

One more started.

"Hissssssssssss."

And another.

"Hisssssssssssssssssss."

Soon the room was full of the sibilant sound of a thousand snakes all hissing and pushing her further. Rosie leaned on the window to escape. She had to get away and she cowered back pushing her shoulders against the cold pane until she heard it crack.

The sound was as loud as a bullet. It rang out across the room. The hissing stopped and the children surged forward.

Rosie overbalanced. Her hands flailed in panic. Desperate to grab onto something. To stop herself and yet there was an inevitability about it. An acceptance. Her hands flew out but she could not touch the children. Would not touch them, these things from beyond. The thought of it filled her with dread. Back and back she toppled as they crowded forward. The glass shattered with a pop and she was falling.

Falling down and down through the darkness, waiting for the crunch of impact. *Shouldn't it be daylight?* The thought crossed her mind just before she hit the ground with a bone jarring crunch.

And then there was darkness.

Her eyes opened to pain and the sound of thunder. It was raining and dark. A flash of lightning lit up the sky. She was lying on the ground and she started to remember. She had been falling.

Shock raced through her, setting her nerves on edge and her skin all a tingle. The scars on her right arm and across her chest tightened and her breath caught in her throat as she sat up.

The children. Where were the children?

Jumping to her feet she scoured the darkness. They were not here, not about and the air seemed to release from her lungs.

Rain poured down, soaking her clothes and hair. Plastering strands to her face and forehead. How long had she been out? Then she remembered it was dark as she fell only that was impossible. It had been light when she entered that bedroom. Light when the children forced her out of the window.

What is happening?

Quickly, she turned in a circle. The house was dark behind her. Menacing and closed it seemed to repel her like water off an oilskin. Round and round she turned. Desperate in the rain and the dark. What should she do? Where could she go? How would she survive this?

Then she thought of Nick, of the priest. It was light enough for her to see in front of her and what other choice did she have. There was no way she was going back into the house. No way was she facing those kids. Yet maybe she could get to his house and then she would be safe.

Setting off toward the back of the house she pushed through the rain. Shivering now as the cold penetrated through her exhausted mind. Would she find his house in the dark?

The sound of a scream rang out behind her. It was desolate and full of pain and it pushed her onward. She would run until she found something, for anything was better than here.

Soon she was amongst the trees. Panting, she pushed aside branches as she raced through the dark. The rain streamed down, and thunder rumbled in the distance. It was so much darker beneath the branches and she feared she would get lost but what did it matter?

On and on she ran as if a hound of hell was panting at her back. Chasing her, hunting her, ready to drag her down and back to that house.

A branch hit her face and she cried out and pushed it aside. The rain was so heavy now. It ran into her eyes and she blinked it away. Ducking and weaving, she ran blindly through the trees and then she saw a clearing. Maybe she had found the priest's home, yet there were no lights.

Coming out of the trees she let out a gasp and slowed to a walk. If she could just take a moment to get her bearings then it would be easier. Only behind her the bushes shook and she could hear something coming through them. Something chased her. Looking back she started to run again. Her foot caught on something hard and she was sent sprawling to the ground. Landing heavily on her arms. She grunted in pain as the wind was knocked out of her. "Jesus!" Her face stopped millimeters from a stone jutting out of the ground.

It was moss covered and old and added to the chill of the rain and the wind... for she knew what it was: a gravestone. Was this where the children were buried? Were they all here in these woods? Had they driven her to this site to find their remains?

Panting heavily she found she couldn't move. Shock had frozen her muscles and she kneeled over the grave. Her head close to the stone then a flash of lightning lit up the sky.

A scream escaped her as she read the faded inscription.

Father Nickolas Aubrey
1725 – 1752

It couldn't be? It couldn't be the same priest, the one who had visited her and yet she knew it was.

Where could I run now?

CHAPTER 11

*R*osie knew she could not go back. Something was happening there and she had to escape it. Logic told her that if she just kept going forward, then sooner or later she would come to somewhere and someone. She would find help and so she carried on in the same direction, tearing back into the trees and running as fast as she could.

Though she knew she would have to slow down eventually she could run for a few miles. Panic and adrenaline meant that she could maybe run for longer and yet tiredness was already sapping the strength from her legs. They ached and felt wooden. Maybe it was a lack of food. She hadn't eaten well since she had got here. When was that? The days seemed to have drifted together and she wondered if it was just a couple of days or longer. When was Amy coming?

The storm seemed to have eased and as she slowed to a walk the rain stopped and all was silent. Holding her breath she listened. Was anyone chasing her?

There was no noise from behind her, no noise at all. Not even the dripping of the water from the trees. At first that seemed creepy. One moment she was running through torrential rain the next it was just so still. *The calm after the storm!* Maybe she was safe, maybe she had outrun her followers. That gave her a boost and she let out a big whoosh of air.

Setting off at a steady walk she searched for signs of life. For lights in the darkness, or the sound of traffic. Anything that would tell her people were close. Anything that could lead her to safety.

There was nothing for as far as the eye could see and so she bit down on her disappointment and just kept walking. Patting her pockets she searched for her phone. Maybe she would have a signal and if not it would give her a welcome light. The phone wasn't there. It must be on her desk. Without it she felt more alone and more vulnerable than she had felt in a long while. For a moment her scars itched. The one on her cheek throbbed and those on her arm and chest burned. It happened whenever she was reminded of her past, whenever she thought about Clive. Only tonight that boosted her. She had survived him against all the odd, she could survive a walk in a wood... forest?

Feeling better she set off at a jog. Moving faster but still being careful that she placed her feet with caution. It would do her no good to fall again. A vision of her as a corpse, sat against a tree with a broken leg flashed into her mind. What was wrong with her and her damned creative mind?

Barely containing her panic, she weaved through the trees always going towards the lightest cloud whenever it peeked through the tops of the branches. It had to be the one that hid the moon and so she had to be going in a straight line. Trees brushed her already soaked arms and covered her in even more cold water. She would have done anything to be warm, dry, and safe. To be sat on Amy's sofa with a big steaming mug of hot chocolate and a blanket.

Up ahead she saw some lights. A beacon in the darkness, they lured her to them. It looked like a single house but it took a weight off her shoulders and she picked up her pace. Weaving through the trees her legs were lighter and faster. She was able to duck more easily and eventually came out of the darkness and approached the dwelling.

As the clouds cleared she let out a wail of anguish. She was back at the house. Back where she started. Only every light in the place seemed to be on. It glowed without warmth. The light mocked her, taunted her almost and she wondered if she dared approach.

How could she be back here? Had she run in circles? That wasn't possible. She was always going towards the moon, of that she was sure and yet... It didn't make sense. For a moment she felt her knees buckle but she would not give in. Would not let it beat her. As she stood wondering what she should do next she saw movement up at the house.

The door swung open and there was something wrong about it. It was a dark wooden door but there was something darker on it. Fear clenched onto her heart and she wondered just how much more she could take. After all the exertion and the shock how much could her poor body cope with before it simply gave up the ghost? For a moment her own thought caused her to giggle and she realized that she was close to hysteria. It was understandable. This had been one hell of a night.

Her eyes flicked back to the woods and the possibility of escape but she knew it was no use. If she ran again then she was sure she would end up right back here. Exactly where she started only more and more tired each time. Maybe she could go in and get her phone. Maybe she could get far enough away to get a signal? Next time she would ignore the woods and try the driveway. It had been a long way to the road but she was young and fit, she was sure she could make it.

Knowing she had no choice, she approached the house. At least inside she could get out of her wet clothes and into something warm and dry.

The closer she got to the house the more dread she felt and the more she wanted to turn and run. When she was just a few feet away she looked down at her arms. They should have been covered in scratches from the nails of the children earlier and from her desperate flee through the woods. Yet her skin was not touched. She still had the ugly puckered scar from the burn, but that was all.

Had she imagined this? Had she imagined it all? With her head down inspecting her skin she walked up to the door and then looked up.

A scream was ripped from her throat.

Pinned to the door was the black cat. Its lifeless eyes stared at her accusingly. Its pink tongue peeked from between sharp white teeth and soft pink gums. Blood ran from the paws that were nailed to the wood and its fur was roughened with dried blood.

The beast's stomach had been opened and its entrails were hanging down like some macabre decoration.

Rosie screamed and the world began to fade. This was it, she couldn't go on. Though she tried to stagger backward her knees buckled and she hit the floor. As she lay before the door she welcomed the blackness that came over her.

At least I escaped for a little while.

CHAPTER 12

*R*osie jerked awake, cold sweat running down her back as she bolted up in the bed. A mournful meow pulled her eyes down to the covers. There, curled up beside her, was the cat. Its sleek back fur looked perfect. For a moment she had a vision of the mottled animal hanging from the door. Then she blinked and could see the cat before her. Its orange eyes chastised her for waking it and Rosie let out a gasp.

It was all a dream, all just a bad dream.

She reached over and grabbed her phone. It was 9.45 and she had overslept. Quickly she checked and the alarm was set. She must have slept right through it.

Stretching, she got out of bed and was pulled to her writing room and the laptop. As she approached she noticed that the laptop was still on. That seemed strange. The screen usually went into sleep mode after ten minutes without activity. It had to have been a lot longer than that since she last sat at the desk. Clicking the mouse pad she flicked to an open document and began reading.

Somehow it was open on a paranormal romance. A girl, Susan, was lost in a time warp where she kept returning to the same spot over and over again. A ghost, Ben, was trying to help her but he couldn't quite break through the vale. He had to watch her being tormented by his brother, an evil spirit out for revenge on her family. As Ben tried to save her, his brother Graham wanted to harm her all because her great, great, grandfather had stolen the woman he loved. Ben found himself falling further and further in love with her and yet to save her he had to destroy his brother. *Could he do it?*

Susan did not know that the two men were spirits until half way through the book. By this time, she had already fallen for Ben. As he saved her life she had to decide whether to free him and never see him again or whether to cling selfishly to his love.

Rosie stopped reading just as she was about to make the decision. That was as far as she had written and she wanted to read the end of the story. It was obviously her own writing and yet it was like nothing she had written before. It was much better and much more real. Was this what her nightmare had been all about? If it were, she would cope with a few nightmares just to finish this story. So, how would it finish?

Closing her eyes, she tried to get inside the characters but nothing would come and then her stomach gave an almighty rumble. She was hungry. When was the last time she had eaten? It felt like days ago and maybe it was. She had been unable to face food after the maggot incident. But there were cans in the pantry and bread in the fridge. *That had to be all right, didn't it?*

Knowing she must eat she set off to the kitchen. The cat followed and she opened it a can of tuna. It meowed its thanks and tucked into the food.

Rosie took the bread out of the fridge and checked it thoroughly before popping 2 slices under the grill. Then she took out some cheese and checked it over too. It looked fine and so she cut some slices while the toast cooked. Then she smothered the bread in cheese and put it back under the grill, while the kettle boiled. Once everything was done she took her tea and toast back to the bedroom.

Eating, she reread the last chapter of the book and tried to get inside the characters once more. Nothing happened. It was as if they wouldn't talk to her and she was getting frustrated. She closed the laptop, took a quick shower and got dressed. Then she grabbed her phone and took her plate and cup back to the kitchen. Her plan was to wash them, make a list of food she needed and then go for a walk. She could walk down the driveway and see how far she had to go until she got a signal. It couldn't be that far and at least if she knew then it would be something to comfort her the next time she had a nightmare.

As she walked into the kitchen she could hear whispering and then she noticed the door in the corner was open. The one with the note on it telling her not to enter. *How had that happened?*

Slowly, cautiously she approached it. As she looked into the door she could see steep steps leading away into a dark hole. About five steps down was a young girl. She looked about eight. Her unkempt hair was ruffled and flat as if she had just got out of bed.

Their eyes met and the girl brought a finger to her lips. The sign for silence.

Rosie nodded.

The girl gave a slight smile and beckoned her to follow.

Rosie looked behind her. There was no one there so the girl must mean her, but could she follow? Could she go down those stairs, and to where?

"Be quick before Matron finds us," the girl whispered.

Rosie nodded and followed her onto the stairs. The door closed behind her and the stairway was plunged into darkness. Rosie felt her chest tighten and the breath catch in her throat. Then a match flared and light filled the passageway. The girl was holding an old-fashioned oil lantern. With a quick nod, she turned away and began to descend.

Rosie wanted to ask who she was and what she was doing but her throat would not work. It was dry and blocked by a lump she just could not swallow.

Down and down they climbed and soon she could hear the sound of rushing water. *What am I doing? Why am I following?* Then she wondered if it was another dream, but when had she slept.

She felt into her pocket, her phone was there. Pulling it out she activated the torch but the light was so harsh that it stopped the girl. They stood on the stairs, so close they were eye to eye.

"Who are you?" she managed to ask.

"My name is Alice, and we must hurry. They want to keep

you. Maybe, I can help you escape but we must hurry before Matron finds out."

Alice turned and carried on going down and down the stairs.

A tingle of goosebumps rose on Rosie's arms, she wanted to go back but she knew she must follow. At the bottom she could see an underground river racing past. There was a path alongside it that headed both left and right. Alice turned left as if she knew exactly where she was going. They came to a room and in front of them was a door.

Alice raised her finger to her lips again and stepped to one side. There was a small alcove filled with shelves, filled with books. Alice scoured the titles raising the lantern high and then stretched up on her tiptoes and pulled down a book and handed it to Rosie.

"Maybe this can help you. Matron is strong, she does not want you to leave. Maybe if you understand you can escape." She handed over the book and lowered her head.

Rosie took the book it was cold and heavy in her hands. Leather lined, the cover felt slimy from the dampness in the air and she almost dropped it. Glancing down she read the title.

"The Sacrifices of RedRise House and the Resurrection of Old Hag."

"What does it mean?" she asked but Alice had already turned away.

She was walking back towards the door and there was a look on her face which spoke of both hope and torture.

Rosie followed and watched as Alice approached the door. It opened as her hand touched the handle and she was pulled inside. Light flickered from the room and Rosie rushed forward to see the young girl surrounded by cloaked individuals. They did not look at Rosie. Maybe they couldn't see her. Though she knew she should turn and run she felt drawn to watch. Somehow she knew this was not happening now. Maybe it was another nightmare and she was safe and sound in bed. Or maybe this was an echo from the past. One she had somehow tuned into. One she could watch but could not interrupt or alter. Though this made sense, she did not think about the book that weighed so heavily in her hands. If she had, she would have felt the full force of terror that knowledge would bring.

Stealthily she crept up to the door.

Alice thrashed desperately as two of the figures lifted her from her feet with practiced ease. With their thick heavy cloaks and dark hoods it was impossible to see any details of their features, just that one was shorter and not as broad. *A woman?*

The room fell silent as they carried Alice to a stone altar and laid her on top. Though it was dark, flickering torches chased ghostly shadows across the walls and Rosie noticed a grisly cache of bones behind the altar. It was piled with human skulls.

Her stomach heaved and her breakfast came back and onto the floor. No one looked her way, no one even flinched and she knew that she was invisible to them. Should she run, should she shout out... what could she do to save this girl, to save Alice?

Alice thrashed against the hands that held her but she had no hope. They were strong and bigger and Rosie knew that they had done this before. As the child tried to escape, they locked eyes. There was a silent plea in the terrified child's glance. Her whites so wide her eyes seemed to fill her face.

"No," Rosie screamed but no one moved, no one even acknowledged that she was there, except for Alice.

The young girl shook her head and gestured with her eyes for Rosie to go.

Frozen to the spot, Rosie could do little but nod her agreement. Somehow she knew that the child wanted her to escape. Maybe it was to bring justice to this place. Maybe if she told of what she had found, if the bones were buried then the child would finally have peace.

In the flickering light, a knife was pulled from the cloak of one of the figures. It flashed in the darkness. Capturing what little light there was and amplifying it like some beacon of hope. Only there was no hope in the terrified child's eyes. Now all they focused on was the sharpness of the cutting edge. It would slice through skin, sinew, muscle and maybe even bone without a moment's hesitation.

Alice was shaking now, her body almost convulsing with fear and Rosie felt her own flesh quake in sympathy. The knife raised high above Alice and then it stopped. It was as if they wanted to prolong the terror, to draw out every second of fear and amplify it to the limit. Poor Alice was still now. Her face showed that she had given in, that all she wanted was for this to end. But it wouldn't would it? How many times had she played out this very same scene?

Rosie wondered if she was the first housekeeper to see this or if there had been others. If so what had happened to them? Had they escaped? No, if they had, then the police would have come... *stop it... this is just a dream*. Her logical mind tried to interrupt but she knew it was lying. This was not a dream; this was real.

Breath held, she waited for the killing blow, just as Alice did before her. Only the figure pushed back her hood and the child's eyes opened even wider.

"Matron," she said.

The woman turned and looked at Rosie, Thin lips curled into a semblance of a smile yet there was nothing warm about the gesture. "You're next," she said just before the knife fell.

Rosie jerked at the blow and let out a mournful scream.

CHAPTER 13

"*N*oooo!" Rosie screamed and tried to run forward to stop the fall of the blade.

It was not possible, she wouldn't make it and yet she had to try. The cellar seemed darker now and the blade hung in the air as she kicked off from a standstill. Heart in her mouth, she reached out with her arms, shouting and screaming to try to make them turn. Something caught onto her legs. Held them tight and she started to stumble, to fall.

Had they got her? Fighting against them, her arms were pinned to her sides. The knife hit the apex and began to fall towards the terrified child. Alice was not moving now. She lay there as if she was paralyzed by the arc of the blade.

Rosie thrashed and fought against the unseen hands as the blade began its fall, sweeping through the air as she kicked and punched her unseen assailants. It was darker now and panic clawed at her throat and crushed her chest. Breath could not get to her lungs as she started to hyperventilate.

The blade hit the child in the heart and she heard a scrape as it hit the stone below. Horror threatened to overwhelm her, to shut her down just as it had Alice. Calm, she knew she had to be calm but how could she when she was held tight? It was no longer about saving Alice. The child must be already dead but she had to escape. She had to run from this house and never come back. Kicking and struggling she felt a little movement and launched herself forward with all she had. Maybe she could escape.

Then she was falling.

Landing with a thump her eyes flew open and it was light. A sharp pain in her hip bone had her scream out in pain and brought her back to reality.

She had been dreaming again. It was just a dream.

Wiping sweat from her face she looked around. She was lying on the floor of the opulent bedroom. The covers tangled all around her. The cat stood at the door, a sad expression on its face.

Rosie laughed. "A dream, just a damned dream."

The cat came across and rubbed against her, meowing to gain her attention. Rosie lifted it up and stroked the animal. It was good to have company and she hugged it close. The cat leaped from her arms at such undignified treatment and went to the door, meowing pitifully.

Rosie ran a hand through her hair and gingerly got to her feet. Her hip was bruised but it held her weight. Looking back at the room she had to laugh again. It looked as if she had launched herself from the bed and landed over four feet away. She was lucky to have not broken anything but at least she knew it was all just a dream. Maybe, if she was lucky, she had written some more of the story.

Was the story real?

She remembered reading it the last time she woke but had that happened? Standing, she found out her phone just as her stomach gave a massive rumble. She was hungry, in fact she was starving. Picking up her phone she looked at the time. It was 9.45 again. That was strange, wasn't that the same time as yesterday? Shaking her head she pushed the fact out of her mind. It must have just been part of her dream, but as she looked at the phone's screen, she almost dropped it to the floor. It was the 5th of September. Somehow, she had lost 2 days!

* * *

A WAVE of fatigue and hunger drove Rosie to the kitchen. She must eat and yet, she did not want to. Was the cheese on toast part of her dream or had she actually eaten it? As she got to the kitchen she spotted the book on the table. It stopped her in her tracks and her blood ran cold. It was large, old, and leather-bound. It was the book from her dream! She remembered the weight of it in her hands, the feel of the leather and the way it was slimy against her skin and her heart missed a beat. How could this be? Where had it come from? If the book was real then was her dream and how had she got back to the bed?

A shudder ran through her as her mind tried to think of a logical explanation. The door in the corner drew her eyes. It was closed and looked like it hadn't been open in years. Should she take a look? What would she do if it opened onto those dark and cold steps? What was going on? Her hand reached out and caressed the leather. It felt just as she imagined. A little slimy as if it was damp. How could this be here when she woke on the bedroom floor? It didn't make sense.

Another grumble from her tummy took her mind away from the book and back to food. It was as if she had forgotten all about last night, all about the dream. Some part of her mind knew this was wrong but it was just a tiny voice in the distance and she pushed it away in her search for sustenance.

Opening the fridge, she saw bread and cheese. They were untouched. She guessed eating it was part of her dream. Pulling them from the fridge she checked the food over. It looked fresh and was void of all creepy crawly bugs. Quickly she prepared herself a snack and boiled the kettle so she could make some tea.

With the snack prepared she sat down at the table and put the plate next to the book. For a moment she was shocked to see it there and then she remembered.

The title read, "The Sacrifices of RedRise House and the Resurrection of Old Hag." It was exactly the same as in her dream. It was about this house, and it was real.

Taking a bite of toasted cheese, she then opened the book and began to read. It seemed to be a journal and was written by a man called Bartholomew Matthews. He had been the butler to a wealthy family but he did not mention their names. There was a wife, husband, and five children three girls and two boys. Though he cared very much for them he loved his own family more and he was devastated when his wife died in childbirth leaving him with a sickly daughter. He named the child Mabel, Mabel Matthews and he doted on her as only a father can. When she was eight years old she developed a sickness, consumption, and gradually faded away.

Rosie was reading the book faster and faster and felt transported back into his world. She could feel his pain and understand his desperation.

I have to do something to save my baby girl, he wrote. *She's all I have left and she is everything to me. I would give my life. I would give my very soul to keep her safe. If there is a God or anything out there that can help me, then I offer myself to save my beautiful Mabel.*

Rosie found she had tears running down her eyes as she read the words. How awful it must be to love someone so much and to not be able to save them. If only it was possible to swap your own life for that of someone else's... How many of us would make such a choice?

She took another sip of tea, turned over the page, and read on.

I did not expect an answer to my prayer and yet I got one. Though I do not know if this is God or something dark and insidious, it is my only hope. Day by day, hour by hour my baby girl fades before my eyes. The pain she is in rips out my heart and I weep for every agonizing breath that she takes. What can I do? Do I accept the arrangement I have been offered? Yet, the presence that came to me feels cold and sinister and still I am compelled to accept the deal. If I do not what sort of father am I?

Rosie found she was reading faster and faster and she took another sip of tea just to slow herself down. Surely this was a story, a fabrication and yet it was written as if it was a journal. As if Bartholomew was telling the tale of what actually happened.

A drawing filled the rest of the page. It showed a man and yet, his features, if you looked at them from a certain angle, were those of a gargoyle. Of a demon?

Rosie stared at the drawing for long moments. It was like one of those computer-generated images that if you looked at it from certain angles you saw one thing and at other angles something else. Yet, this was pencil drawn, or at least it looked to be. How could something so intricate and complicated be made out of something quite so simple? Slowly, she turned the page, as she did the energy in the room seemed to change. Behind her the kitchen door slammed and she jumped in her seat as adrenaline sent spikes of fear through her veins. The door opened again and slammed shut. Once more it did the same thing but this time it was accompanied by other doors in the house. The cacophony of doors opening and closing, slamming against the jam and then flying back filled the house with a roaring chaos that was like a physical assault. Rosie cowered in the chair, her hand on the book. Her eyes searched the room and yet found nothing.

The doors' banging got faster and faster, the noise rising with the speed, and at the same time the air hummed with electricity. Rosie knew she must escape that she must get out of here but she was too scared to move. Where would she go anyway? She could not get through the door without being trapped in the wooden jaws which would break bones at the very least.

Maybe it was the book? She should close it, but before she could, she was picked off the chair and sent spiraling across the room. The force, as she hit the wall, knocked the air from her lungs. Gasping for breath, she was sent back across the floor. Scraping and sliding, she slammed into the other wall, hitting her head with such force that darkness began to descend.

Once more she was picked up and thrown, only this time she

could see the children in the room. She hit the wall at head height. Crushing pain lanced into her shoulder before she slid down to the floor and the noise was gone.

The pressure eased up and she thought it was over. Yet, huddling together in the center of the room were the children. They looked just as she remembered; only now, they were frightened. They clung to each other. Wide eyes searched the corners and pleaded for her help.

What were they afraid of?

CHAPTER 14

*P*anting desperately, Rosie lay on the floor and stared at the children. This couldn't be real, it just couldn't. Yet the pain in her back and arms, the pain in her head and neck told her that it was. She would be bruised tomorrow, if she made it to tomorrow.

The children were staring towards the cellar door and she let her eyes followed theirs. The door opened and first one and then another cloaked figure came through it. The first one was tall and broad the second smaller, lighter. It was impossible to see their features and she imagined the worst; they had to be hideous beneath the hoods. Then she remembered the demon from the book. Was this what had come to get her? Would she join the children? To be here in this house for all eternity.

"Matron," the children whispered together and huddled even tighter.

The pressure of fear pushed down on her chest, crushing her lungs. Rosie couldn't breathe. All she could do was stare at those two figures. The corner where they stood appeared darker. It was as if the very light was afraid to shine on them and it added to her fear.

Her lungs screamed for oxygen. Her vision was going dim and her legs were too weak to hold her. Part of her knew she must escape, that she must get away from here. Yet how could she, when she couldn't even stand?

The two figures moved into the room and threw back the hoods from their cloaks. Their faces were just as bad as the empty darkness that had been there before. Their skin was stretched tight over gaunt cheeks bones. Their eyes were sunken deep into their face. Thin lips were stretched over pointed teeth designed for ripping and tearing.

She tried to remember a prayer and yet, nothing would come to mind as the figures turned to look at her.

Gasping for breath, she slithered along the floor, hutching away from them as efficiently as she could. Her chest ached, her lungs screamed and still she could not breathe. Panic was like the weight of a car forcing down on her chest and crushing her lungs. Until she pulled herself out from under it, she could do nothing but succumb to its devastating weight.

Then she remembered the Lord's Prayer. The most common prayer, the one everyone knew and it gave her a touch of comfort. She was able to draw in a big breath of air and felt much better as she started to repeat it out loud.

"Our Father who art in heaven, hallowed be Thy name. Thy kingdom come, Thy will be done, on earth as it is in heaven."

The two adults let out a mighty roar and stepped toward her. Once more the pressure in the room grew and she had to stop praying and gasp for breath. It would have been so easy to just stop. To slump against the wall and to let whatever was coming come but she would not. Her eyes were drawn to the children. There was hope on their faces. Hope and encouragement and it was directed toward her.

"Give us this day our daily bread, and forgive us our trespasses, as we forgive those who trespass against us, and lead us not into temptation, but deliver us from evil. Amen."

The two cloaked figures stopped before her, their faces curled into a snarl. Dark eyes pinned her to the spot. Fear snatched the very air from her lungs and she felt the room chill to freezing. A shiver ran through her and she held her breath waiting, waiting for them to do something. They stared at her. Their dark eyes shrouded in shadow. Their thin lips parted. They didn't seem to move, to breathe; they didn't seem to be alive.

Just when she thought she could take no more the sound of her mobile ring snapped her back to normality.

The phone's ringing!

The figures stood there, staring, and then with a slight upward curl of their lips, they were gone. Rosie looked for the children. They were staring at her. There was something in their eyes. Something they were trying to tell her. Before she could understand they too faded away to nothing and she was left with just the ringing of her mobile.

Rosie fished the phone out of her pocket and pressed it to her ear. "Hello, hello," she spoke desperately. Praying that this was real. That she finally had contact with the outside world.

"Hi Rosie, it's Amy here sorry I missed all your calls."

"Amy, oh my God Amy. It is so good to hear your voice. Please, please come and pick me up straight away. There is something terrible going on here and I am so frightened. Please come get me today, now, for I do not think I will survive another night."

"I'm so pleased to hear you're enjoying it," Amy answered.

"Amy can't you hear me I'm frightened and terrified please help me."

"I know sometimes people can be silly but I'm pleased you're enjoying yourself," Amy said. "I know I was supposed to be there tomorrow but I just called to say I won't make it... oh that's good... yes, I will only be three more days I hope you don't mind."

"No, no please Amy you must come collect me tonight or send someone or ring the police or anything, just get me out of here please." Tears were running down Rosie's face as she tried to make Amy understand. It was obvious that her friend heard a completely different conversation. Maybe the spirits were interfering, maybe she was going mad but somehow she had to find a way to make Amy understand.

"Amy!" she shouted at the top of her lungs. "You have to come save me or I fear I will be dead by morning."

"That is fantastic. I'm so pleased you are writing again. Didn't I tell you this house would be perfect? Now I have to go, you have fun and I will see you in three days."

The phone went dead in her hands. Rosie tried to call her back, then to dial the police, only she no longer had a signal. Had the spirits done this just to torment her? Or was it one more figment of her imagination. She no longer knew and yet she knew she had to get out of there.

Making a decision, she picked up the phone and stood up. The house was deadly quiet, the air still and a little heavy. It didn't matter. She was leaving and she was never coming back.

Yet, as she made the decision... she wondered if the house would let her go.

CHAPTER 15

*R*osie was surprised that it was easy to walk out of the house. She got to the door the cat meowed and seemed to be willing her onward.

"Are you coming with me?" she asked.

Wise orange eyes stared up at her and seemed to tell her to go and to not look back. So she opened the door and stepped out. Pausing, she held him and stared back at the cat. He looked at her, looked at the outside, then turned slowly, then like the hunter he was, ran back into the house.

Rosie closed the door and set off across the driveway. Her feet crunched on the gravel and sank deep into the stones. It was hard-work, hard going and she had a long way to walk. Though only the part near the house was graveled she still knew it would take some time before she reached the road. What she needed to know was how long until she could get a signal. Then she remembered the cab driver. Maybe he hadn't been questioning her past, maybe he understood this house. She knew his number was in her mobile and as she walked she tried to dial him.

No signal.

Trying to keep in mind what had happened, she looked out at the countryside. The grounds of the house were really magnificent. This side, the front of the house was like a country park. Long open spaces of grassland dotted with magnificent trees.

It was very different to the back of the house, which was more sinister. A dark and dank forest surrounded the far side. Yet, as she walked down this drive the sun warmed her arms and she wondered if those things really had happened to her. Absentmindedly, she reached up to her head and felt a bruise. There were other bruises she could feel as she walked. Something had happened to her. Either she needed help or she was in trouble. It didn't matter which, she was not going back.

Every 5 to 10 minutes she tried to ring the cab driver or the police or Amy. Each time she couldn't get a signal and so she walked on again. She had been walking for over an hour and was tired and achy and yet the countryside hadn't changed. Surely she should have come to the main road by now. If not it had to be anytime soon.

Stopping, she tried to phone again and once more it flashed to tell her that she had no signal. Up ahead, the drive curled around a copse of trees and she hoped that when she got to the other side she would finally reach the road and get a signal.

As she rounded the corner she dropped to her knees and let out a wail of despair. There in front of her, less than 300 yards away was the house. Somehow she had looped the estate and was back exactly where she started.

Sitting on her knees, she let her tears fall. It wouldn't let her leave. They wouldn't let her leave. Would she ever survive this?

* * *

Rosie sat at the kitchen table, a tuna sandwich untouched before her. Occasionally she sipped at her tea while she read as much of the book as she could. It was hard reading. A heart-wrenching tale of joy and then desolation as the father realized exactly what he had done. What he had given up for a short time with the daughter he knew.

The demon came to me again tonight. It had the audacity to visit the bedchamber as I tended to my dearest Mabel. The sound of her tortured breathing plays like the bellows at the blacksmith shop. Each draw of breath could be her last. I am selfish for I wish it to go on and yet I wish it to stop.

The demon asked me if I had made a decision, and I have. I told it I would give my life and my soul to see my girl healed. For her to be healthy and to have a long and happy life before her. It was a hard decision and I know my Mabel would not want this but I cannot let her die. Not like this, not so young and not in so much pain. When I told my visitor it seemed to make the demon happy and yet there was something... some smile that I did not quite trust. I believe I am being duped and yet what can I do?

The master paid for the physician to come and see my Mabel today. The man told me to make arrangements. What use was he? So, I wait and will see what I can do for my girl.

The demon says he will come back tomorrow and tonight I will pray. I will ask the Lord to help me make the right decision. I will ask him to forgive me for I cannot let my baby die.

Rosie fought back tears. One thing she had never told anyone, the one thing that played on her mind and kept her awake at night was the fact that she could not have children. It was one of the reasons that Clive was always angry with her. When she found out, she told had him. In her mind she expected his support and yet he treated her as if she had betrayed him. That was when she should have really left and yet having just lost the chance to have a family she could not let go of the one person she cared about the most. Yet, this was not the time to be dwelling on her past, not if she wanted to survive, to have a future.

Since she had been back, so far the house had been quiet and nothing else had happened. She had put all the downstairs lights on and had some tunes playing on her phone. Adele was currently singing about *Rolling in the Deep*. It made the house feel less empty, less threatening, and yet she knew it was just a foolish mind trick.

Taking a sip of her tea, she made a few notes on what she had just read. It was late, past 11 at night, and yet she did not think she would sleep. The more she learned, the greater chance she had of surviving this.

Part of her wished that Amy was here now and another part wished that her friend would stay well away. Would the spell that was cast upon her that prevented her from leaving this place, be gone when Amy turned up? Or would they both end up trapped in this hell? It tormented her mind and yet the hope and wish to see Amy kept her going.

Rubbing her eyes she turned back to the book and began to read once more.

Nothing really came of my prayers. It is as if the Lord has abandoned me. Maybe it is what I deserve, after all I have offered up my very soul for the safety of my Mabel.

Now I wait, with just a single candle burning, for the demon to arrive.

There is always a stench of rotten eggs, of sulfur, just before he appears and I can smell it now. My stomach flips, my heart pounds, I know that I should run from this beast and yet he is my only hope. This is the first time I have left my Mabel's side in some days. Yet I do not want to do this in front of her. Part of me thinks that she would be disappointed in me and that I could not bear.

Rosie looked up as she heard a noise. It was just the cat. He slinked into the room and rubbed against her leg. Rosie scooped him into her arms and set him on her knee. Stroking the silky fur and feeling comforted by his presence she continued to read while Adele sang about *Turning the Tables*. It seemed appropriate.

The smell of sulfur entered the room and then he was here. This time he made no pretense of walking through the door but simply appeared before my eyes. My heart was beating so fast I felt it may burst from my body and yet I must keep going for just a little longer.

"What would you do to save your daughter?" the creature asked.

A lump formed in my throat. I had to swallow before I could speak and I fear that he will think I have changed my mind. Sweat was running down my forehead as I tried to get the words out. Can I see amusement in the ugly face before me? I thought I could, and it frightens me. At last I can speak. "I will do anything," I tell it. "I will give you anything I can, I will do anything I can. Just ask and it will be yours. If you want it, you can take my soul."

The Demon laughed and I felt a chill run through me.

"I will do this for you," he said. "I will make your girl well, I will let her live a long, long life; all I ask for is her soul."

I felt as if my heart has been crushed and ripped from my chest. I could almost see it in the creature's clawed hand. It takes one last beat before he squeezes it and the very life of me runs from between its gnarled fingers. "You have asked for the one thing that I cannot give," I tell the creature. "How can I give away a soul that is not mine?"

"Then go to your daughter, for she will be dead within the hour. I will be listening throughout this her last night; all you have to say is, 'I agree,' and she will live."

The creature was gone. It just disappeared from before my very eyes and left me with my guilt, my fear, and my tears.

Rosie had to stop reading. The story was horrifying and she felt such sorrow for the father who had to make such a terrible decision. How could he watch his little girl die and yet how could he pay such a terrible price? She wanted to close the book, to go to sleep or even just rest, yet somehow, she knew that her life depended on the knowledge she would gain here.

Her throat was dry and she was feeling cold. So she took a sip of tea and found it had long gone cold. While the kettle boiled, she grabbed a jumper and then made herself a fresh pot. Refreshed, she sat back down to read and learn, and hopefully to find a way to escape this place.

As I sit by my dear Mabel's bed, her breath that was once so labored and so terrible to hear is now so faint. It is also slowing down and yet I can see the pain she is suffering. Just a few moments ago her eyes opened and pleaded with me. I do not know if they plead for life or for death and it tears my heart apart. I'm holding her hand now willing her to fight or to let go I no longer know which is for the best.

"Help me daddy," she pleads. "Please just make the pain go away."

Her skin is so pale and she gasped as I touched her forehead. I can take no more. God forgive me for what I am about to do. Letting go of her hand I close my eyes and say, "I agree."

CHAPTER 16

I agreed, I said the words and the creature appeared before me. The smile on its face was as cold as a winter's morning and it sent chills deep into my bones. Only that does not matter for it reached out and touched my Mabel and instantly her breathing eased. She is sleeping now. The lines and stress have gone from her face and her color is coming back. I know I have done the right thing and I cannot wait to hold my girl in my arms when she is healthy and strong.

The next two pages of the journal were blank. It was as if he had left them and had intended to come back and write something else. Why had he not done so? It did not matter....she had to keep reading so she turned the page, hoping that the story would have a happy ending.

It has been two days since I made the deal and at first, I was very happy. I did not feel the need to write in this book. Or maybe I was too ashamed to do so. At first my Mabel was wonderful. She smiled so much and laughed and thanked me for all I have done. Yet, today I saw her push one of the children down the stairs. If I had not caught him, little Jeremiah would have been badly hurt. Why would my girl do such a thing? Sometimes when I look at her I wonder if she is my girl anymore. Perhaps the creature already took her soul and perhaps what he left behind is not the best of her.

Rosie felt her chest tighten. She should have known this was coming and yet she always wanted the happy ever after. It was hardwired into her and she could not think that the story would not end well. For several days, nothing happened and Bartholomew began to relax again. His joy was short lived.

I believe my Mabel is fighting whatever possesses her and I believe she is losing. Now, I wonder what possessed me to put my little girl through such torture. For surely, what she has become is worse than death itself. She is now a cruel child who thinks of no one but herself.

Rosie read on and on and on and could not believe the awful circumstances that Bartholomew had gotten himself into. With each turn of the page she wished that he would succeed and yet, to do so, he had to kill his own child. This was the most awful story she had ever read and she wanted to slam the book closed and walk away but she felt compelled to read on. Maybe, just maybe her own life depended on it.

It has been six weeks since I made the deal. For most of them I have regretted it, and now I fear for my life. Tonight, I will commit the most heinous crime known to man. I will kill my own child.

Rosie turned over the page, she hated that she wanted to read about how he managed to kill the child for maybe that was her way to survive. Yet there were just two words on the next page and they appeared to be written in blood.

You Failed.

The next few pages were empty there were just marks, just

red smudges on the parchment and nothing more. Then the writing changed and someone else took up the story.

My name is Nicholas Aubrey and I am a local priest. I arrived at the house today to find the family and all the children, as well as my good friend Bartholomew Matthews, dead. It appears they have been heinously murdered. I was so overjoyed to find that Mabel survived. Yet I do not know how, but I have to thank the Lord that at least someone made it out of this awful massacre.

Rosie read on as the priest described what he found. Everyone's throat had been cut, just like she saw the girl, Alice, in her dream and all the children who pushed her from the window. The cat was disemboweled and hung on the door. Just like in her dream. Only this was not the end. Mabel hadn't survived... she had committed the massacre and it wasn't long before Nicholas found out what had really happened. In an act of bravery he tried to exorcize the demon from the child and to lay the lost souls to rest. He wrote down exactly what he was going to do as well as the prayer that he would use to chase the demon from the child's body, but that was the last entry he made.

Once more, Rosie turned over a page to see those two words written in blood. *Was it Nicholas's blood this time?* Somehow she knew it was.

You Failed.

Rosie turned back and reread all he had written. She reread the exorcism prayer and committed it to memory. Maybe this was all she would get from the book; it wasn't much, but it was a start.

There were a number of blank pages in the book after that, but then the writing started again and once more it was a different hand that penned the words. The person was unhinged and the words did not make sense. Perhaps it was Mabel fighting the demons or perhaps the demon just didn't care, Rosie got little from the next 30 or 40 pages.

Then gradually the demon began to chart its life. It spoke of power and control and how much it, she, loved those things. Apparently she could affect people's minds and bend their will to her own purposes. Was that what was happening to her? Rosie guessed it must be.

As she read on, the demon knew that it needed to take sacrifices and it became bored on its own so it set up an orphanage. Apparently it was easy to do. It appeared that in those days there were no regulations and people were often desperate to get rid of children. Such a thought threatened to drown her in sorrow. With each turn of the page she read of hurt and pain inflicted on the children. It tore at her heart but she must keep reading. She must stay strong, there had to be something within the book to help. If not, then why had Alice lead her to it?

Every ten years or so, Mabel started to suffer with her breathing. It looked like the consumption came back. To overcome it, she had to take a life, to make a sacrifice to the demon. Each time she did, her power grew. Then there came a number of people who found out. Rosie was glued to the pages, hoping to find a new way to destroy the spirit. Shock halted her eyes on the page. They did not want to destroy her and called Mabel "Old Hag." What they wanted was to worship her and bask in her power. So she developed followers who would help her kill and torture.

Rosie kept reading but her sense of unease was growing. So she skipped to the end of the book and found out that Old Hag was bored with staying at this house. She wanted out but she could not leave. Rosie turned the page back and forward looking for more information but there was nothing.

How could she stop this evil from leaving? How could she escape herself?

She had not learned much but she had the prayer, and also from the priest, she knew that salt would weaken the spirits and the demons.

Rosie was as prepared as she could be. Now all she could do was wait. She had no way of calling the spirits to her. She must wait for them to make a move. Somehow she knew it would be tonight. There was a feeling in the house of tension, of a presence. She could not work out if it was friendly or harmful.

Time ticked past so slowly and fatigue was like a weight on her shoulders, dragging her down into the promise of rest... of sanctuary. Yet, the last thing she wanted to do was sleep, for she knew that Mabel, Old Hag, would take over her mind if she succumbed. Somehow, she knew that if she slept tonight that she would never wake up again.

To keep herself awake, she went to her desk. There she opened a blank document and typed out the exorcism prayer. She put a salt container on her desk and she fetched her Bible from her bag. She had carried it around for years and yet she had not looked at it since the incident with Clive. Right now, Clive was the least of her worries.

With that done, she expected something to happen but the minutes ticked on and on and she began to feel fatigue. A yawn opened her mouth and closed her eyes. It muddled her brain and lulled her to rest.

Shaking her head she fought the feeling. Still, nothing had

happened and yet she could feel someone watching her. The hair on her arms rose as goosebumps traced across her skin. It was harder to breathe, as the room seemed to vibrate with unseen energy and yet it did not feel threatening. Could Alice be here?

"Alice, is that you? Can you help me?"

The temperature dropped in the room and she could see a darkness against the wall. With her heart pounding in her throat and her breath held she watched, as Alice gradually came into view.

"Can you help me?" she asked again.

Alice shook her head and started to fade.

"No, please don't go. If you can't help me, can I help you?"

As she watched, the figure seemed to grow in strength. She was still translucent but appeared more real and tears formed in her eyes. Blinking them away, she floated across the room towards Rosie. Anguish crossed her young face as she tried to talk yet it seemed that she could not speak the words so she pointed at the exorcism prayer.

"This," Rosie said, as she picked up the paper. "Will this help you?"

Alice nodded and Rosie heard words in her head.

I do not think you will be strong enough to destroy her. Every one of us here gives her strength. We do not want to, we want to rest. Maybe, if you say the prayer with meaning and with fortitude then maybe we can rest. If you can send enough of us away, then maybe you have a chance. Just keep reading the prayer and put your soul, your faith, and your heart into believing that she... that we all... must leave.

"Thank you," Rosie said and watched as Alice faded and was back at the other side of the room. She was fainter now, transparent and she shimmered in and out of view.

Rosie felt hope. She had a plan and as she watched, more of the children appeared. They did not look threatening this time. In fact, they looked as if they were waiting for Christmas or for some amazing treat. There was excitement in their eyes. They held hands and whispered to each other. If she could do this then she would have done some good and she could have her happy ending.

Filled with new purpose and a feeling of strength, she picked up the paper and began to read the exorcism prayers.

CHAPTER 17

*R*osie took a deep breath and centered her mind. She wanted the children to find peace. She wanted to release them and she concentrated on that thought as she read out the prayers.

"Visit this place, O Lord, we pray, and drive far from it the snares of the enemy."

It felt wrong. The children were not her enemies and yet she could see from the smile on Alice's face that this was what they wanted.

"May your holy angels dwell with us and guard us in peace, and may your blessing be always upon us; through Jesus Christ our Lord. Amen."

The pressure in the room increased and she felt as if she was being squeezed. As if the air had gone out and there was no longer enough to breathe. She could see from the faces of the children that they were frightened and she knew that Mabel, the Old Hag, was behind her. What should she do? Should she turn around and concentrate on the stronger spirit or should she try and remove some of her power by carrying on reading out the prayers.

It was too much, she needed to see what was behind her and she faltered in her reading and began to turn. Panic crossed Alice's face. Rosie stopped and looked at Alice. She was so young and so brave, Rosie nodded she would do this for them, for the children. Ignoring what was behind her she looked at the children and carried on with her plan. What good could she do against such a powerful creature? No, she had to stick to the plan and she continued to pray. The next part was easy for it was a simple releasing prayer. Yet the urge to look behind her was more than she could take. Her shoulders tensed and she flinched with each word, excepting to be slammed from behind, or worse.

"In the Name of Jesus, I rebuke the spirit of Jeremiah Patterson. I command you leave this place, without manifestation and without harm to me or anyone, so that He can dispose of you according to His Holy Will."

As she said the words, she watched the smallest of the boys before her step forward. A smile broke out on his face, and like the sun breaching the clouds, it filled her with warmth. That one sign of human kindness chased away a little of her fear and filled her with a sense of achievement.

He mouthed the words *thank you* and then he was gone.

She did not know how she knew his name but it had come to her just as she had said the prayer.

There was a roar behind her and something hit her back. Tumbling against the desk she stood and faced the spirit.

The hooded creature was just feet behind her. The hood hid her face and the taller man was at her side. Though she could not see her features she could feel the anger and hatred that rolled off her. It thickened the air and filled it with the fetid odor of rotten flesh. Rosie gagged and fought down the urge to vomit. She had to stay calm. Matron, Mabel, or Old Hag, was angry and she was afraid. Nothing else mattered, she had to get rid of her. Then she could give these children peace, and if she did that, she believed she had a chance to save herself.

"Christ, God's Word made flesh, commands you. Be gone, Satan, inventor, and master of all deceit, the enemy of man's salvation. Unclean and evil beast, hear the Lord's words and be gone."

Matron threw back her hood and dark eyes blasted Rosie with loathing. The look was like a physical force, pushing her back and she wanted to run. To turn and flee from this place but she couldn't. Where would she go?

A pitiful sound pulled her eyes back to the children. She had to help them if it was the last thing she did.

"I cast you out, unclean spirit; in the name of our Lord, Jesus Christ, be gone from these creatures of God."

A strong wind roared toward her and knocked her off her feet. She was slammed into the wall with a resounding crash and the pain in her shoulder threatened broken bones.

Turning from Matron she concentrated on the children. This was her power, remove the Matron's support base and she would have a chance. Only she had suffered a major blow and she had a long way to go.

"In the Name of Jesus, I rebuke the spirit of Mary Patterson. I command you leave this place, without manifestation and without harm to me or anyone, so that He can dispose of you according to His Holy Will."

A small girl smiled at her before disappearing.

Matron screamed and the room became a whirlwind of flying objects. Rosie ducked down and covered her head with her one good arm. When she felt something cold touch her hand. Peeking out from beneath her arm she saw Alice holding the salt.

Taking it she understood and she picked herself up and battled against the wind. Slowly she managed to make her way across the room to Matron and she threw the salt at her. At first Matron just gave her a look of pure hatred. Rosie threw again and then the spirit was gone.

Rosie collapsed back onto the floor, gasping. Before she could catch her breath, Alice was back and she knew that she must not rest. This respite gave her time to weaken the spirit and she had to take it.

"In the Name of Jesus, I rebuke the spirit of Lydia Patterson. I command you leave this place, without manifestation and without harm to me or anyone, so that He can dispose of you according to His Holy Will."

Rosie did not know where the names were coming from but as she said the prayer a name came into her mind and the corresponding child stepped forward. There were over two dozen of them. More than she realized before and Alice seemed to be the leader. She protected the children, holding their hands and pushing them forward if they were reluctant to go. Her sweet smile was strong and warming and she nodded often to show her approval.

Rosie was exhausted. Each time she read the prayer it

drained energy from her. It was as if she was giving a little bit of herself to help the children cross over and she wondered just how much more of it she could take. What would happen when Matron came back?

There was no time to dwell on such things, for that way led to madness and fear. If she were to do this she must be calm, quick, and determined. Each child she sent to peace reduced the spirits power and increased her chances and yet she was so tired how could she ever wish to fight her?

Rosie started the prayer again, "In the Name of Jesus, I rebuke the spirit of Martin Johnson. I command you leave this place..."

The air chilled in her lungs and the pressure on her chest took the very breath from her. Rosie dropped to her knees and clutched onto her chest. The pressure was intense. It squeezed her lungs until they screamed. On her knees she choked and coughed, desperate to draw breath. Just as darkness began to settle over her she felt a hand on her shoulder. Looking up, she saw Alice.

"Just breathe, it is all in your mind. We will help you," the girl said in her mind.

Rosie dragged in a desperate breath and nodded. Looking up she could see four figures wearing the heavy dark cloaks. Her vision was still blurry and she could not make out their faces, even though their hoods were down. Then she could see that they surrounded a smaller figure. They must be her acolytes, the malevolent people who had given up their souls to worship this creature. How could she face such evil and win?

Rosie tried to stand but was blasted off her feet with a gust of fetid air. Knocked back, she slammed into the wall. The impact was bone crunching and knocked the wind from her lungs. For a moment she felt her eyes close and blackness was a welcome friend. It would take her away to a world of rest and recuperation. Slowly she let it take her and relaxed into the dark. A hand shook her shoulder and then slapped her face.

Rosie jerked awake to see Alice before her.

"Do not sleep or you will be hers," the young voice said in her head. "You will be a lost soul forever if she gets inside of you."

Rosie nodded and shook her head to clear it. The acolytes were approaching her and she knew that this would be the last battle. Could she win?

CHAPTER 18

*A*lice was by her side offering support.

This incensed the spirits and Rosie could feel the hatred as they rushed toward her. Raising her hand, she threw the salt and chanted the prayer.

"Christ, God's Word made flesh, commands you. Be gone, Satan, inventor, and master of all deceit, the enemy of man's salvation. Unclean and evil beast, hear the Lord's words and be gone."

As the salt touched the black robes, curls of smoke rose into the room and the acolytes stopped. Their hoods were raised but she could sense their doubt. It was as if she could understand their minds. They had been promised eternal life and suddenly they were vulnerable and it shocked them to their core.

Was she winning?

Again, she said the prayer and walked forward tossing salt over the cloaked figures. "Christ, God's Word made flesh, commands you. Be gone, Satan, inventor, and master of all deceit, the enemy of man's salvation. Unclean and evil beast, hear the Lord's words and be gone."

The one to her left dissolved. It was as if the salt was acid that burned through the heavy cloak and then into the flesh below. The creature screamed in a most inhuman way and yet the more it burned the more it appeared to become what it once was. As if the pain burned away the evil and stripped it back to the person it had once been. One moment it writhed in agony and the next the face cleared, smoothed and dark eyes gained peace and then it was gone. The other figures were backing slowly away.

Filled with confidence Rosie walked forward and tossed more salt.

"Christ, God's Word made flesh, commands you. Be gone, Satan, inventor, and master of all deceit, the enemy of man's salvation. Unclean and evil beast, hear the Lord's words and be gone."

She pushed every ounce of energy she had into the prayer and filled it with the intense desire to see the spirits gone. They melted before her eyes. As if struck down by a holy white fire sparking from the grains of salt.

Now, she was face to face with matron and she could feel the joy of the young girl beside her. This had been a long time coming and Alice was rejoicing. Yet, Rosie could see the look on the spirit's face. She was not afraid and that scared her. What did she know? Or maybe she also wanted peace after all these years.

"You will not destroy me!" Matron roared. "I am old and eternal and I have traveled this path many times before. Run now and I will let you leave... if you stay I will consume you and use your body for all eternity."

There was silence and Matron pointed to the door. For a moment Rosie almost turned and ran. Something about the old woman's face told her that she actually had the choice. That this time she would escape. Only as she looked at the door she looked past Alice. The young girls face crumpled into a look of pure despair and yet she nodded. Alice would encourage her to go, to save herself even though it would leave her and the rest of the children in torment. Rosie knew she could not do that. No, she was in this until the end and she would have her happy ever after. She would save all the children and she would send this evil bitch back to the hell she came from.

Quickly she walked forward throwing the salt and shouting out the prayer, "Christ, God's Word made flesh, commands you. Be gone, Satan, inventor, and master of all deceit, the enemy of man's salvation. Unclean and evil beast, hear the Lord's words and be gone."

Mabel stepped back in shock and seemed to fade.

"Our Father who art in heaven," Rosie prayed. "Hallowed by Thy name. Thy kingdom come."

Matron was fading. It was not the same as the other spirits. She did not burn or sizzle as they had done.

"Thy will be done on earth as it is in heaven."

Instead she seemed to fold in on herself. Shrinking before their eyes. Becoming smaller and fainter.

"Give us this day out daily bread, and forgive us our trespasses, as we forgive those who trespass against us."

Rosie felt her spirits soar and continued walking toward the shrunken figure. She was winning; she would survive this. Once more she threw salt and the woman bowed over before her.

"Lead us not into temptation, but deliver us from evil. For thine is the kingdom, the power and the glory forever and ever."

As she walked towards Matron the older woman faded away to nothing.

Rosie had won.

She dropped to her knees and put her head in her hands.

"Amen," she whispered and then burst into tears. She had done it. She had survived and all she wanted to do now was curl up on the floor and sleep.

A gentle hand touched her shoulder and she looked up to see Alice smiling up at her. This wasn't over. She still had to see that all the children were given rest.

"I haven't forgotten you," she said and sat up. "Just give me a minute."

The gentle voice appeared in her head. "There is no rush. We can wait another night. Sleep now and we will watch over you. Tomorrow night is time enough to lay our souls to rest."

Rosie nodded and stumbled to her feet. She walked across the office and to the opulent bed in the other room. For a moment something nagged at her mind but she pushed it away and fell onto the bed. Before she could even adjust her position she was asleep.

CHAPTER 19

*R*osie jerked awake and sat up in the dimly lit room, her heart pounding. With her hand clutched to her chest, she listened and tried to make sense of what had woken her. It was hard to remember but she had been dreaming. In her dream she was fighting and she was losing.

There was nothing here.

She let out a long breath and relaxed against the headboard. It had all been a dream. Closing her eyes she tried to calm her pounding heart and catch her breath. Yet there was something wrong with her cheek. It felt different, stiff, no not that. It just felt wrong. Thinking that it was probably just how she lying but knowing she wouldn't sleep until she had taken a look she crawled out of bed and stumbled to the bathroom.

As her feet touched the floor her back and hip ached. It had not been that long since she had taken a severe battering. The bumps and bruises were letting her know about it.

Maybe that was what was wrong with her face. Maybe it was just a bruise and yet still, she felt drawn to the mirror. She had to see what the problem was.

Pulling on the cord, she flooded the bathroom with light. The gray room had never looked so somber. The paint so dull it cloaked the room in shadow. Now she knew she had to be imagining this. Looking for problems where there were none. So she walked to the sink and ran some water. Then, she looked up at the mirror and her face.

Fear traced a cold knife down her spine and then rammed it into her heart. The hairs rose on her arms and her breath froze in her throat. The left side of her face was distorted.

Her hand reached out to touch it; the skin felt course, dry, wrinkled. As she watched, it was as if that side of her face was aging rapidly. The skin tone slackened. Her cheek dropped and deep crow's feet appeared around her eyes. Wrinkles spread across her cheek and lines appeared etched deep into the skin.

Rosie's mouth fell open, still she could not breathe.

What was happening?

She wanted to turn away. To run back to the bed and crawl under the covers to hope that by morning this would be gone, that it was all a dream.

Instead she reached down with both hands and scooped water from the sink. Splashing it over her face.

The right side felt exactly as she thought it would but the left side felt different. It was almost as if the skin was not real, as if it was not hers. How could this be?

In her mind she tried to call Alice. The young girl had helped her so much and maybe she could help her now. Nothing happened, just that strange half face in the mirror.

Maybe this was just a dream and she had to wake up. With her right hand she pinched her left arm.

"Ouch."

The pain was real and still nothing changed.

At last she could draw in a breath and found she was gasping for air. Breath after breath she pulled into her lungs but still she wanted more. The panic was taking hold, closing her airways once more and weakening her. Closing her eyes, she willed this to be gone, willed it to be back to normal. As she opened her eyes, the wrong face stared back at her.

Once more, she lifted her hand to touch her cheek. Tentatively she traced two fingers over the crow's feet and down her skin. It felt so strange and she pulled her hand away. Only in the mirror the hand continued to trace downward.

Rosie let out a gasp.

The left eye and the left side of her face curled into a smile... no... it was not a friendly gesture, this was a mocking, cruel motion, it was a sneer.

Stunned, Rosie reached up to touch her face. The hand in the mirror moved with her, for a moment she thought she had imagined everything. It was just her mind playing tricks on her. Yet as her fingers touched her cheek the hand in the mirror turned. She could still feel the wrinkled skin and yet she could see those very same fingers reaching out towards the mirror.

How could this be?

"I still have power," the face in the mirror said. "You may have gotten rid of some of my strength but much of it still remains and now they will help me destroy you. See?"

The fingers looked different. Like her cheek, they were older. The joints twisted and swollen with arthritis. As they touched the glass it rippled like the surface of a lake and then the hand burst through and pointed behind her.

The breath left Rosie's lungs and she turned around to see that she was surrounded by the children. There were at least ten of them and once more they wore the feral visage of desperate animals. They were angry, controlled, and braying for her blood.

Rosie searched for Alice but she was not amongst the crowd. How she hoped the girl had escaped but she did not think it was possible. Then she saw her, standing near the door of the bedroom.

"Alice run!" Rosie shouted. "Maybe I can set you free but keep away from her."

Alice hesitated on the threshold. Dithering on the spot, as she wondered what was the right thing to do.

"In the Name of Jesus, I rebuke the spirit of Alice Cotton."

There was a roar from behind her and Rosie turned back to the mirror just in time to see a figure step from the glass.

It was Matron, the woman in the cloak. She was bent and wrinkled but as Rosie watched she straightened up and smiled in a way that turned Rosie's blood to ice.

"Who are you?" she asked.

"You know," the voice said. "I gave you the opportunity to leave and you turned it down. Now you will be mine."

"I command you leave this place," Rosie shouted putting all her focus on letting Alice go but she could not take her eyes off the spectacle in front of her.

The old woman was changing. The skin became firmer, the cheeks more rounded. The wrinkles smoothed out as she watched. Gradually she seemed to straighten up. It was as if the kinks in her spine were dissolving and she was becoming younger before Rosie's very eyes. Only that wasn't all that was happening.

Rosie knew she had to keep on with the prayer but her mind was blank as the woman staggered towards her and put her hands around her throat. Ice cold fingers squeezed onto her windpipe and the face began to change. It was morphing, flexing, dissolving and reforming and Rosie could not take her eyes off it.

As her lungs began to burn and her throat craved for just one breath of air, the figure that was squeezing the life from her became her. She was looking at a mirror image of herself. Staring into her own eyes as her own fingers squeezed the very life from her body.

Only the new her wasn't solid. At times the figure would blink and she got the chance to draw in a breath. It seemed to happen at regular intervals and she watched and waited until she was ready for the next one.

As the fingers dissolved and loosened on her neck she stepped back. Ignoring the pain and the desperate urge to breath she shouted with all she had, "Alice go, without manifestation and without harm to me or anyone, so that He can dispose of you according to His Holy Will. Amen."

Rosie turned to the door. Alice was looking at her with a smile on her face and yet there were tears in her eyes. She had found peace and she faded away but she was replaced by Matron wearing Rosie's body.

Matron thrust her hands around Rosie's neck before she could move and was squeezing again.

Rosie could feel the blackness settling on her but she knew she had to fight. So she timed it carefully and as the hands loosened she stepped to the left. She was free for a second and she drew in a deep breath before starting the prayer again.

"In the Name of Jesus, I rebuke the spirit of..."

The hands were back around her throat before she could say a name. It had been strange but each time she tried to lay the soul of one of the children to rest, their name came into her mind and she knew that the next child was Shaun Bedford, but she could not speak the words. As the hands tightened around her throat she tried to think them but everything was going black.

"You are not strong enough," she heard her own voice say.

Be gone unclean beast, Rosie thought, but there was nothing left.

"No, not this time."

Rosie felt herself fall and could see her own eyes looking down at her. Her own hand over her mouth and nostrils and then the figure was gone.

Had she won?

CHAPTER 20

For a moment Rosie felt sweet relief. She took in a huge breath and felt the sweet air fill up her lungs. The urge to choke was strong. How she wanted a drink to ease the soreness on her throat but the children were crowding around her once more. Their faces were wild, their eyes wide and their lips curled back over sharp teeth in a snarl.

Rosie tried to swallow. Once she could speak she would say a prayer for each of them and she would release them and yet the way they looked at her sent a fission of fear into her heart.

Why were they still like this? Why was it as if they were still under Matron's control?

"Because I'm still here," a voice said in her head and then Rosie understood.

Matron had not gone. Somehow she was inside her and she was about to have the battle of her life. A searing pain sliced into her brain. It was like hands ripping and clawing at her cerebral cortex and she had no way to fight against it. Each rip caused a spike of pain and a little bit of her will was torn away. She was being clawed out of her own body and she could not resist.

First Matron ripped out the part of her brain that controlled speech. Without that she couldn't formulate thoughts and so she couldn't say the exorcism even in her mind.

Rosie felt her body go weak as the part of her brain that controlled her spinal cord was shredded. Now something was replacing her. Something was filling up the place where she had once been and she wanted to ask a question but didn't know what it was.

Then the pain stopped, everything stopped and she was just a cell floating on a dark ocean of nothingness.

A voice came out of the sky, maybe it was a God, or maybe it was the universe. She didn't know what those things were but it spoke to her. As she listened she felt a cold darkness and a feeling of such despair. What had she done?

"I have been trapped in this house for so long but I have learned my lesson. If I killed you, I gained another acolyte for my army but I was still trapped here. This time you will be my host. You will be my way into the world and all the delights that have been hidden from me for so long. Thank you Rosie, for I couldn't have done this without you."

Rosie knew she had lost but she also felt her self returning. Her mind was not lost it had just been suppressed. Now, Matron was securely in control of her she allowed her to be once more and Rosie began to wail inside her own mind. She could see what Matron had planned. How she intended to kill and torture and to spread her reign of terror as far as she could and Rosie would not be able to stop her.

* * *

I<small>T WAS</small> two days later when Amy arrived.

"How are you doing?" she asked as she bounded into the house all full of smiles and pulled Rosie into a hug.

Matron smiled but Rosie was screaming, shouting and rattling on the inside of her skull. Anything to make Amy see the danger before her. Only none of it could be seen.

"I want to leave," Matron said. "I contacted the owners and they say it is fine. I'm just to lock up and post the key."

"Don't you want to hear the good news?" Amy asked and gave that cute little smile that said she was teasing.

Matron was impatient, "Can't it wait?"

"Hey, Rosie, what is it?"

Rosie felt Matron crawling through her memories and she tried to shut them down. Tried to make it hard for the spirit to learn from her but it was no use.

"Sorry, I've just been having nightmares. About Clive. I think he may have found me."

Amy laughed and pulled her into a hug. "That's just it. He's been arrested. They found him trying to get back into your old place and he's in jail. You're finally free."

Inside her prison Rosie started to cry. She would never be free, not ever again."

"That is such good news, now let's go celebrate I could kill for a decent Mocha."

"You and me both," Amy said.

Soon they were in Amy's car and as she drove away Rosie looked back at the house. What was currently beautiful fell rapidly into a state of disrepair. The garden was filled with weeds. The house lost roof tiles and the windows were broken. The front door was hanging off the hinges and the place looked as if it had been abandoned for decades. Maybe it had, maybe it was only Matron keeping the place going. Surrounding the door were the children. They tried to follow but each time they got more than twenty feet from the door they would disappear and snap back to the front of the house. It looked like they would be trapped there forever.

"I will release you one day," Rosie said in her mind.

"No, you won't," a cold voice replied. "You will stay here and watch me murder your best friend."

Rosie screamed and shouted and raged at the prison that was her mind but the only response she got was a deep and evil chuckle. She had lost and the world would pay for her foolishness.

* * *

I HOPE you enjoyed The Haunting of RedRise House. It was a fun book to write and gave me a lot of sleepless nights. Read on for more books and a way to get FREE Advanced Copies of books from me.

Caroline Clark

CALLED FROM BEYOND

COMING SOON

6th July, 2018

Country Road,

Yorkshire.

England.

11.59 pm.

Mark stared out through the windscreen at the dark and twisty road ahead. He stifled a yawn. "Probably should have taken up the offer to stay the night." The long drive back to civilization slowly ate away at his concentration. Taking his eyes off the road, he turned to face Alissa.

She had her feet curled up on the seat next to her and her eyes were almost closed. "Mmm, probably. It was good to see them again," she said, pushing her long blonde hair back from her face.

He loved to see it when it fell in whispers across her pale

skin. It was so fine and silky to the touch and, right now, he just wanted them back in the hotel so he could hold her. These bleak and lonely roads were no place for a couple of city kids like them and he couldn't wait to get back to the noise and bustle of Leeds.

They were staying at a hotel in one of the small villages— make it a bit of a romantic night as well as a reunion—but now he wished they hadn't. Maybe he should have taken her away somewhere not just down the road from their house?

"It *was* good," he said, pulling his eyes back to the road. "They both looked so healthy. And the food? Mmmm. Amazing."

"Don't I know it." Alissa's bright smile contrasted with the dreamy quality her eyes still held. "That stroganoff was so creamy and delicious. I think that's why I'm so sleepy. I'm way too full."

Mark laughed. "Or perhaps a few too many glasses of red wine?"

"You're only jealous because it was your turn to drive." She stuck her tongue out and her green eyes danced with laughter.

"Funny, that." He tried to put a stern expression on his face. "It's always your turn to drive on the way there and mine to drive back."

"Yeah, I like the way that works out." She snorted a giggle and closed her eyes again. "Perfect, if you ask me."

Mark laughed and turned back to the road. Fatigue was like a heavy blanket and his eyes just wanted to close. He quickly rubbed a hand through his short brown hair. Though he was no longer enlisted, he never let his hair grow more than a finger. He unwound the window and let a cool breeze travel across his scalp. The fresh draft much more invigorating than the cold air from the blowers. Right now, he needed something to bring back his concentration. At least another twelve miles laid between them and anything that even remotely resembled an A road.

"Do you think they made the right decision?" Alissa asked.

"You mean moving out here?"

"Yeah, it's a long way from London."

Mark thought about it. He missed their friends so he wanted to say no, then he thought about how much they laughed and smiled tonight. "We made the move for your job, what was it... three years ago now?"

"We moved to a city."

"Leeds is a big city but it's not London and you adapted."

Alissa grumbled. "I know, but right out in the country and into that old rundown house?"

"It looked pretty nice to me. I think they're happy there and that's all that counts, right?" It hit him hard that he wanted things to change. That she wanted more from the relationship was no secret and right now he understood. He turned to look at Alissa.

That pretty smile he loved so much. She was a picture to behold with perfect skin, a heart-shaped face, and the biggest green eyes you ever did see. A splattering of freckles danced across her nose and more tiptoed down her arms.

Sometimes he tried to count them when she was asleep.

They had been engaged for a year now, but when he proposed, it had simply been a stop gap for him. He never intended the engagement as a prelude to marriage and he knew that stank.

She gave everything to him, was always generous and loving. His best friend.

How could he treat her like that? Right now, he knew he wanted to marry her, but he also knew it was the wrong time to set the date. He had to make it more romantic.

She deserved that.

"Keep your eyes on the road," she gently admonished.

Nodding, he turned back. The headlights hardly cut through the gloom and he eased up on the accelerator, slowing the car just a touch. The beams of light shone into the ether as they topped a brow and then dropped to the tarmac as they began to descend. The dark and twisted trees lining the road on their right sucked the light from the moon. To their left, the road sloped alarmingly away and more trees dotted the grassland along with the occasional sheep. He hated the fact that sheep were on the road. Where were the fences? Surely farm animals were supposed to be fenced in fields for safety?

"Penny for them?" she said, bringing him back to the moment and more pleasant thoughts.

"Why don't we stay another night? We could come for a walk on the moors, have a nice romantic meal and then just chill a little."

Alissa laughed, a silky sound that stroked down his nerves and filled him with love. "When I look out the window all I can hear is *'stay on the road—keep clear of the moors.'*"

Mark laughed. What other woman would get his favorite

film? An old one, for sure, but still the best. "Maybe we could find a pub called the Slaughtered Lamb?"

Alissa chuckled. "No, that would be too freaky."

"Mark!" her voice was high pitched and cut through the joy like a knife through silk. Green eyes were wide and staring, and her mouth dropped open.

The world slowed as he turned his head back to the road.

The headlights barely penetrated the soft mist in front of them, but he clearly saw a woman standing there. A white dress fluttered around her thin frame and her face seemed carved in granite. *Frozen in an eternal scream.*

Mark yanked on the steering wheel and jerked the car to the left. He tensed, waiting for the crunch as steel hit flesh and broke bones—a sound he knew well—and a memory of war flashed into his mind. Broken flesh. Blood. A world of fear and pain.

Pushing those thoughts aside, he trusted his reactions were good. The car turned instantly. Only, it shouldn't have been quick enough. But there was no crunch, just a flutter of white across the windscreen, and then it was gone.

They left the road and tore across the grass. Like a turbo powered shopping trolley they careered down the hill out of control. Trees loomed out of the black as the headlights went out and so did the power. The car plunged into darkness. The engine had died but nevertheless hurtled down the hill. Mark pulled left and right, avoiding a sheep and then a tree. Everything lurched out of the dark and was on them so soon. His right foot pressed hard on the brakes but nothing happened. He pushed the gear lever into first. The car should have slowed considerably but it didn't. Before he could do anything else, another tree loomed out of the darkness and engulfed them.

This time, the crunch was bone wrenching as they ground to a halt. He instinctively reached out to his left to steady Alissa, but it was too late. They both flew forward until they hit their seatbelts.

Another crunch and breaking glass showered him. The car finally rolled to a stop.

Mark's ears rang and his chest hurt. His training kicked in and he assessed the situation and his own injuries. Nothing but cuts and bruises. His neck was jarred and his knees had impacted with the steering column. They ached like hell, but the seat belt had saved him from worse injuries.

The car seemed stable but how was Alissa? Leaves cut out the moon and he could only make out shapes. As his eyes adjusted to the dark he searched for Alissa and reached for his phone. The seat belt was in the way. He couldn't reach the clasp. Fighting down panic, he methodically searched for the catch.

Alissa! The thought was threatening to drive him into a panic but he knew that would not help. Although his chest ached from the seatbelt strain, he managed to cough out, "Babe, are you okay?" So far, he couldn't hear her moving but that could just be the compression from the bang that had affected his ears. Many a shell blast had given him a permanent ringing in his ears, but now they were almost screaming at him. Why was it so dark? Why had the lights gone out? He didn't know but there was no time to think about that now. They had to get out of the car.

At last, he managed to free the seat belt and tipped forward. Reaching for his phone, he pulled it from his pocket and shook it twice. The torch light lit up and he almost let out a wail of grief.

Alissa was looking at him. Her eyes were glassy. Not the glassy darkness of death. This was the shine of shock, of trauma. He had to act quickly.

"Hey, baby, how are you?" He spoke gently but as matter of factly as he could.

Her eyes lashes fluttered. She was awake and aware. That was good. For a moment, the woman on the road came to mind, but he pushed the thought away. They had missed her, but it didn't matter. Even if he had hit her, there was nothing he could do now. *Deal with what you can*, that was what his training told him. *Don't go looking for more trouble.* Once he had gotten Alissa out of danger, he would search for the woman.

He checked Alissa for injuries and a groan nearly escaped him as panic threatened to overwhelm.

She was leaning back against the seat. Her face looked fine, just pale, but that wasn't what scared him so.

A tree branch jutted out of her left shoulder. The gnarled and green wood had pierced straight through her light green top, through flesh, blood, and sinew, and into the car seat.

Think!

For a moment, he grasped the branch sticking out from her shoulder.

Alissa let out a groan of anguish and he pulled his hand away.

Blood was leaking from the wound, but it was just a trickle. If he pulled the branch clear, he would be able to move her from the car but the wound would bleed much more quickly.

151

If she had severed an artery, she would be dead before he could do anything.

First aid kit!

He sprang from the car and battled the branches of an oak tree. They crumbled easily with each strike. The old and weary tree could topple onto the car any second now. Alissa would be crushed. Each groan and creak of the limbs surrounding him forced a bead of sweat onto his forehead.

He pulled up the coordinates of where they were on his phone then dialed for an ambulance as he moved around to the back of the car.

Mark popped the boot and immediately spotted the first aid kit strapped against the wheel arch.

"Emergency services, which service please?"

"Ambulance," he said as he carried the first aid kit back inside the car. He went back to the driver's side as he could see her door was buried deep beneath the branches and he didn't want to waste time digging her out or risk disturbing the hovering tree.

With the phone clamped between his neck and shoulder, he opened the kit and crawled back into the car.

"Help me?" Alissa pleaded and he could see the glint of tears on her cheeks.

"I'm here, baby, you'll be out of here any minute."

"Ambulance, what's your emergency?"

Mark explained as he packed around the wound with gauze.

"I suggest you leave her where she is and go back to the road to help flag the ambulance down," the operator told him.

For a moment, Mark thought about it. But he couldn't leave her. The tree groaned above him, how long would it hold? Would he get her out before it came crashing down?

Alissa's breathing was ragged now. Panicked.

Hearing her in such pain tore out his heart.

"I can't leave her and I have military training. Just get to these coordinates," he said and then he dropped the phone back into his pocket.

"You have to get me out of here." Alissa grabbed hold of his hand.

Her grip was weak, her fingers cold.

"I will, baby, but you must be patient."

Leaves rustled overhead and a branch fell, bouncing off the top of the car. They were out of time. He needed to get her out of there, but he'd have to pull the branch from her shoulder to do so. The angle was wrong from the driver's seat. If he did it from here, he would open up her wound even more. If he did that he doubted he'd be able to stop the bleeding in time.

She'd bleed out in his arms.

If he could get in through the passenger door, then it would be a cleaner jerk. The branch would come out at the same angle as it had entered her shoulder and he could staunch the flow more easily, and then get her from the car and possibly even tie off the artery.

"Just hold still a moment," he said and pulled her fingers from his.

Panic gave her strength. Despite her small size she clung on so desperately that it was hard to get free.

"I will only be a moment," he whispered against her ear then gently kissed her hair. The blonde tresses were no longer silky but wet with blood. Had she hurt her head?

There was no time to think about it, so he left the car and fought his way to the front and through the branches. A large branch was wedged against the door, and he kicked at it to break it free. The tree above them shuddered and rained down sticks and smaller branches. Something groaned and cracked and still the door was wedged tight. He kicked at the branch with all his might, knowing that it was a choice between time and force. Too much time and the tree might collapse on top of them, too much force and he might hasten that outcome. His foot hit the branch and it slid across the door. The tortured metal screamed but the branch fell away.

He pulled on her door, but the impact had bent the metal. His breathing was ragged, and the fear inside him fought like a wild horse for freedom but he reined it in. Feeling around the door, he found the dent and then kicked the panel to clear the frame.

Alissa let out a scream of pain.

Mark felt as if he had been stabbed in the gut, but he had to keep going. Grasping hold of the door, he pulled with all he had. For a moment nothing happened and his muscles protested at the effort. His eyes adjusted to the darkness as he worked to free the door.

With one last gargantuan effort it sprang open and he hauled it back as far as it would go. Alissa's eyes were drawn down, her mouth grimacing in pain. That was a good sign. If she could feel, then she hadn't gone into shock yet and there was hope.

He fought around the door. He was about to lean into the car when a ripping sound dragged his gaze upward. A thick branch tore free from the trunk and fell down, and down. The massive limb smashed through the windscreen and slammed into Alissa's face with a dull thunk.

As warm wet splashed his face, he screamed, certain he'd never be able to stop.

To find out when Called From Beyond is released join my newsletter you will also receive The Black Eyed Children FREE.

Never miss a book
Subscribe to Caroline Clark's newsletter
for new release announcements
and occasional free content: http://eepurl.com/cGdNvX

25th April 15 82

The basement of the cage.

Derbyshire.

England.

3:15 am.

Alden Carter looked down at his shaking hands. The sight of blood curdled his stomach as it dripped onto the floor. For a moment, his resolve failed, he did not recognize the thin, gnarled fingers. Did not recognize the person he had become. How could he do this, how could he treat another human being in this terrible way and yet he knew he must. If he did not, then the consequences for him would be grave. For a second he imagined a young girl with a thin face and a long nose. Her brown hair bounced as she ran in circles and she flashed a smile each time she passed. The memory brought him joy and comfort. Brook was not a pretty girl, but she was his daughter, and he loved her more than he could say. He remembered her joy at the silver cross he gave her. The one that he was given from the Bishop, the one that cost him his soul.

Rubbing his hands through sparse hair, he almost gagged at the feeling of the crusty blood he found there. How many times had he run those blood-soaked fingers through his lank and greasy hair? Too many to count. It had been a long night, and it was not over yet. This must be done, and it was him who had to do it.

Suddenly, his throat was dry, and fatigue weighed him down like the black specter of death he had become. A candle flickered and cast a grotesque shadow across the wall. Outside, the trees shook their skeletal fingers against the brick and wood house and he closed his eyes for a moment. Seeing Brook once more he strengthened his resolve. The trees trembled, and the wind seemed to whisper through their leaves, tormenting him, telling him that he was wrong but he would not stop. Could not stop. Taking a breath, he felt stronger now, and with a shaky hand, he picked up an old stein and took a drink of bitter ale. It did not quench his thirst, but it gave him a little courage. He must do this. He must go back down to the cage and finish what he had started, for if he did not Brook would not survive and maybe neither would he?

The kitchen was sparse and dark and yet he knew he was lucky. The house was made of brick as well as wood. It was three stories' high and was bigger than he needed. This was a luxury few could afford. As was the plentiful supply of food in the pantry and work every day. The Bishop had been kind to him, and he knew he had much to be grateful for. Yet, what price had he paid? As the wind picked up, the trees got angry and seemed to curse him with their branches. Rattling against the walls and making ghostly shadows through the window. Alden turned from them and up to the wall before him. The sight of it almost stopped his heart and yet he knows he must go back down to the cage. If the Bishop found him up here with his job not done, then he would be in trouble... Brook would be in trouble. A shiver ran down his spine as he approached the secret door. Reaching out a shaky hand he touched the wall. It was cold, hard and yet it gave before him. With a push, the catch released and the door swung inward. Before him was a dark empty space. A chasm, an evil pit that he must descend into once more.

Picking up the oil lamp, he approached the stairs and slowly walked down into the dark. The walls were covered in whitewash, and yet they did not seem light. Nothing about this place seemed light. Shadows chased across the ceiling behind him and then raced in front as if eager to reach the hell below. Cobwebs clawed at his face. These did not bother Alden, he did not fear the spider, no, it was the serpent in God's clothing who terrified him.

With each step, the temperature dropped. He had never understood why it was so much colder down here. Cellars were always cool, but this one... with each step, he felt as if he was falling into the lake. That he had broken through the ice and was sinking into the water. Panic clenched his stomach as he wondered if he would drown. The air seemed to stagnate in his lungs, and they ached as he tried to pull in a breath. It was just panic, he shook it off, and was back on the stairs. His feet firm on the stone steps he descended deeper and deeper. He shrugged into his thick, coarse jacket. The material would not protect him, of that he was sure, but he pushed such thoughts to the back of his mind and stepped onto the soft soil of the basement floor.

There was an old wooden table to his right. Quickly, he put the oil lamp on it. Shadows chased across the room. In front of him, his work area was just touched with the light, he knew he must look confident as he approached the woman shackled to the wall. Ursula Kemp was once a beauty. With red hair and deep green eyes. Her smooth ivory skin was traced with freckles, and she had always worn a smile that had the local men bowing to her every need. Seven years ago she had married the blacksmith, and they had a daughter, Rose. Alden felt his eyes pulled to his right... there in the shadows lay a pile of bones. A small pile, the empty eyes of the skull accused him. Though he could not look away from that blackened, burned, mound... the cause of another stain on his soul. Bile rose in his throat, and the air seemed full of smoke. It was just his imagination, he swallowed, choked down a cough and pulled his eyes away. Blinking back tears, he turned and looked up at Ursula. Chained to the wall she should be beaten, broken, and yet there was defiance in her eyes. They were like a cool stream on a hot summer's day. Something about them defied the position she was in. How could she not be beaten? How could she not confess?

"Confess witch," he said the words with more force than he felt. Fear and anger fired his speech and maybe just a little shame. "Confess, and this will be over."

Ursula's eyes stared back at him cool, calm, unmoving. She looked across at the bones, and he expected her to break. Yet her face was calm... her lips twitched into a smile.

Alden's eyes followed hers. The bones were barely visible in the dark, but he could still see them as clear as day. A glint of something sparkled in the lamplight, but he did not see it. All he could see was the bones. Sweat formed on his palms as if his hands remembered putting them there. Remembered how they felt, strangely smooth and powdery beneath his fingers. *Ash is like silk on the fingers...* a sob almost escaped him, and for a second he wanted to free Ursula, to tell her to run... and yet, if he did then the Bishop may turn him and Brook into a heap of ash like the one he was trying to not look at.

In his mind, he heard the sound of a screaming child, the sound of the flames. Smelt the burning, an almost tantalizing scent of roasting meat. Shaking his head, he pushed the thoughts away. Now was the time for strength. Biting down on his lip, he fought back the tears and turned to face her once more.

"You will not break me," she shouted defiantly. "Unlike you, I have done no wrong. Kill me, and I will haunt you and your family until the end of time."

Alden turned as anger overrode his judgment, striding to the table he picked up a knife. It was thin, cruel, and the blade glinted in the lamplight. Controlling the shaking of his hands, he crossed the room and plunged it into her side. For a second it caught... stopped by the thickness of her skin. Controlled by rage, he leaned all his strength against it and it sliced into her. Slick, warm blood poured across his fingers. "Confess, confess NOW," he screamed spraying her face with spittle.

A noise from above set his heart beating at such a rate that he thought she must hear it. It pounded in his chest and reminded him of his favorite horse as it galloped across the fields.

The Bishop was here.

Without a confession, he was damned, but maybe he was damned anyway. Maybe his actions doomed him to never rest, yet he must save his daughter, he must save his darling Brook.

As he heard the door above open, panic filled his mind, he must act now, or it would be too late. Then he saw it in her eyes, Ursula knew what was coming. She knew she would die soon and yet she did not fear it. Maybe she thought she would meet her daughter, that they would be together again. He did not know, but the calm serenity in her eyes chilled him to the bone.

In a fit of rage, he struck her on the temple. The light left her eyes, her head dropped forward, and she was unconscious, but it no longer mattered… he had a plan.

"You have confessed," he shouted. "You are a witch. By the power of the church, I sentence you to death, you will be hung by the neck until you die."

Before the Bishop reached him, he pulled back his hand and slapped her hard across the face. The slap did not wake her, but the noise resounded across the cellar. As the Bishop stopped behind him, he felt an even deeper chill. This man had no morals, no conscience. Alden knew what he had done was wrong, but he did not care. If it kept his family safe, he would sacrifice any number of innocents, and yet his stomach turned at the thought of what was to come.

"You have your confession," the Bishop's voice was harsh in the darkness. "Let us hang her and end this terrible business."

* * *

Ursula woke to the feel of rough, coarse hemp around her neck. As her eyes came open, she felt the pain in her side and knew it was a mortal wound. The agony of it masked the multiple injuries she had received over the past few days.

Alden was holding her. Hoisting her up onto a platform which was suspended over the rail of the balcony. The rope tightened as he placed her feet on the smooth wood and fear filled her. This was it, she knew what was coming, and yet she shook the fear away. To her side, the Bishop stood, a lace handkerchief in his hand as he dabbed at the powder on his face. Blond hair covered a plump but handsome visage, with good bones and a wide mouth, but his eyes… they were gray and hard. The color of a gravestone they could cut through granite with just a look. Amusement danced in them, or maybe it was just the lamp flickering. It could not provide nearly enough for her to really tell, and yet she knew.

Alden moved away from her and turned to the Bishop. There was a hardness to him too. His lips were drawn tight enough to make a thin line, but he could not fool her. Alden was afraid, and she pitied him, pitied the days to come. For her, it was over. Death would be a sweet release, but for Alden, it had only just begun. As he pushed the table, she looked down to the floor below. The lamp did not light more than half way, and it seemed that she would jump into a bottomless pit. If the rope did not stop her… then maybe she could fly. Down deep she hoped she would soar, away from pain, away from fear and safe in the knowledge she held.

If only.

The moon came from behind a cloud and shone through the window at her back. Its light cast shadows through the branches of a large, old oak tree. Sketchy fingers coalesced on the far wall, and her heart pounded in her chest.

Was this a sign?

A welcome?

The shadows danced and then formed and appeared to be a finger pointing to her doom.

It was time.

Before Alden could push her, she stepped out into nothing.

Read The Haunting of Brynlee House now always FREE on kindle unlimited http://a-fwd.to/2UiiG7w

PREVIEW: THE HAUNTING OF
SEAFIELD HOUSE

30th June 1901

Seafield House.

Barton Flats,

Yorkshire.

England.

1. a.m.

Jenny Thornton sucked in a tortured breath and hunkered down behind the curtains. The coarse material seemed to stick to her face, to cling there as if holding her down. Fighting back the thought and the panic it engendered she crouched even lower and tried to stop the shaking of her knees, to still the panting of her breath. It was imperative that she did not breathe too loudly, that she kept quiet and still. If she was to survive with just a beating, then she knew she must hide. Tonight he was worse than she had ever seen him before. Somehow, tonight was different, she could feel it in the air.

Footsteps approached on the landing. They were easy to hear through the door and seemed to mock her as they approached. Each step was like another punch to her stomach, and she could feel them reverberating through her bruises. Why had she not fled the house?

As if in answer, lightening flashed across the sky and lit up the sparsely furnished room. There was nothing between her and the door. A dresser to her right provided no shelter for an adult yet her eyes were drawn to the door on its front. It did not move but stood slightly ajar. Inside, her precious Alice would keep quiet. They had played this game before, and the child knew that she must never come out when Daddy was angry. When he was shouting. Would it be enough to keep her safe? Why had Jenny chosen this room? Before she could think, thunder boomed across the sky and she let out a yelp.

Tears were running down her face, had he heard her? It seemed unlikely that he could hear such a noise over the thunder and yet the footsteps had stopped. *Oh my, he was coming back.* Jenny tried to make herself smaller and to shrink into the thick velvet curtains, but there was nowhere else to go.

If only she had listened to her father, if only she had told him about Alice. For a moment, all was quiet, she could hear the house creak and settle as the storm raged outside. The fire would have burned low, and soon the house would be cold. This was the least of her problems. Maybe she should leave the room and lead Abe away from their daughter. Maybe it was her best choice. Their best choice.

Lightning flashed across the sky and filled the room with shadows. Jenny let out a scream for he was already there. A face like an overstuffed turkey loomed out of the darkness, and a hand grabbed onto her dress. Jenny was hauled off her feet and thrown across the room. Her neck hit the top of the dresser, and she slumped to the floor next to the door. How she wanted to warn Alice to stay quiet, to stay inside but she could not make a sound. There was no pain, no feeling and yet she knew that she was broken. Something had snapped when she hit the cabinet, and somehow she knew it could never be fixed. That it was over for her. In her mind, she prayed that her daughter, the child who had become her daughter, would be safe just before a distended hand reached out and grabbed her around the neck. There was no feeling just a strange burning in her lungs. The fact that she did not fight seemed to make him angrier and she was picked up and thrown again.

As she hit the window, she heard the glass shatter, but she did not feel the impact. Did not feel anything. Suddenly, the realization hit her and she wanted to scream, to wail out the injustice of it but her mouth would not move. Then he was bending over her.

"Beg for your life, woman," Abe Thornton shouted and sprayed her with spittle.

Jenny tried to open her mouth, not to beg for her own life but to beg for that of her daughter's. She wanted to ask him to tell others about the child they had always kept a secret, the one that he had denied. To admit that they had a daughter and maybe to let the child go to her grandparents. Only her mouth would not move, and no sound came from her throat.

She could see the red fury in his eyes, could feel the pressure building up inside of him and yet she could not even blink in defense. This was it, the end, and for a moment, she welcomed the release. Then she thought of Alice, alone in that cupboard for so long. Now, who would visit her, who would look after her? There was no one, and she knew she could never leave her child.

Abe grabbed her by the front of her dress and lifted her high above his head. The anger was like a living beast inside him, and he shook her like she was nothing but a rag doll. Then with a scream of rage, he threw her. This time she saw the curtains flick against her face and then there was nothing but air.

The night was dark, rain streamed down, and she fell with it. Alongside it she fell, tumbling down into the darkness. In her mind she wheeled her arms, in her mind she screamed out the injustice, but she never moved, never made a sound.

Instead, she just plummeted toward the earth.

Lightning flashed just before she hit the ground. It lit up the jagged rocks at the base of the house, lit up the fate that awaited her and then it was dark. Jenny was overwhelmed with fear and panic, but there was no time to react, even if she could. Jenny smashed into the rocks with a hard thump and then a squelch, but she did not feel a thing.

"Alice, I will come back for you," she said in her mind. Then it was dark, it was cold, and there was nothing.

Read The Haunting of Seafield House for $0.99 for a limited time but always FREE on Kindle Unlimited http://a-fwd.to/6UXsowk

ALSO BY CAROLINE CLARK:

Based on a real haunted house - Brynlee House has a past, a secret, it is one that would be best left buried.

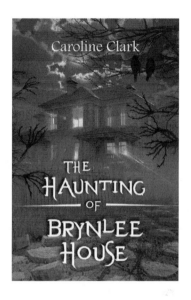

Read The Haunting of Shadow Hill House http://a-fwd.to/5HMB7UX for FREE on Kindle Unlimited or on Amazon Prime for a limited time only

ABOUT THE AUTHOR

NEVER MISS A BOOK.

Subscribe to <u>Caroline Clark's</u> newsletter for new release announcements
and occasional free content:
http://eepurl.com/cGdNvX

* * *

Want Books for FREE before they hit Amazon?

Would like to become part of Caroline's advanced reader team? We are looking for a few select people who love Caroline's books. They will receive a free copy of each book before it is released. We will ask that you share the book on your social media once it is released and give us any feedback on the book. You will also get the chance to interact with Caroline and make suggestions for improvements to books as well as for future books. This is an exciting opportunity for anyone who love's the author's work. Click <u>here</u> to find out more details

* * *

I am also a member of the haunted house collective.
Why not discover great new authors like me?

Enter your email address to get weekly newsletters of hot new haunted house books:

http://.hauntedhousebooks.info

HTTP://.HAUNTEDHOUSEBOOKS.INFO

Caroline Clark is a British author who has always loved the macabre, the spooky, and anything that goes bump in the night.

She was brought up on stories from James Herbert, Shaun Hutson, Darcy Coates, and Ron Ripley. Even at school she was always living in her stories and was often asked to read them out in front of the class, though her teachers did not always appreciate her more sinister tales.

Now she spends her time researching haunted houses or imagining what must go on in them. These tales then get written up and become her books.

Caroline is married and lives in Yorkshire with her husband and their two white boxer dogs. Of course one of them is called Spooky.

You can contact Caroline via her facebook page: https://www.facebook.com/CarolineClarkAuthor/

Or via her newsletter: http://eepurl.com/cGdNvX

She loves to hear from her readers.

❀ Created with Vellum

24797223R00107

Printed in Great Britain
by Amazon